I0663157

The Kyoto Man,

A

PULP SCIENCE FICTION NOVEL

"Extravagant Fiction Today—Cold Fact Tomorrow"

By

D. Harlan Wilson.

Book Three of the Scikungfi Trilogy.

THE FIRST EDITION

_____

Edited by Dr. Master Master Stanley Ashenbach Esquire.

BOWIE:
Printed by RAW DOG SCREAMING PRESS in Maryland,
and for STICK FIGURE INCORPORATED in Bliptown.

MMXII.

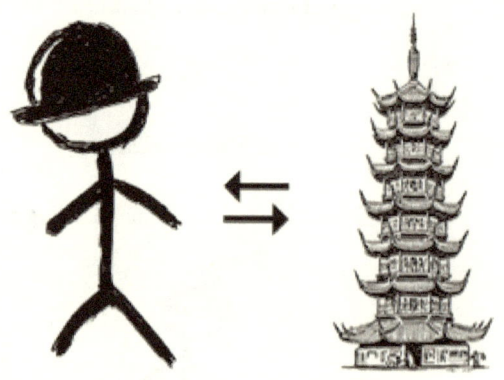

Acclaim for the Works of D. Harlan Wilson

Codename Prague

"In this second installment of his scikungfi trilogy (after *Dr. Identity*), Wilson ups his creative ante with new bursts of stream-of-cyberconsciousness prose to rival Gilbert Sorrentino (*Mulligan Stew*) and William Burroughs (*Naked Lunch*) … With the cinematic feel of *Pulp Fiction* and a sound slap at modern culture, this should attract a select audience that appreciates metafiction and pulp action." **Library Journal**

"This novel is from the wild edge of science fiction, in the tradition of Philip K. Dick's *The Three Stigmata of Palmer Eldritch*—fast, smart, funny, and full of a scarily plausible vision of just how weird things could get if we take our biological fate into our own hands." **Kim Stanley Robinson**

"This intense mixture of giddy activity, cyberpunk essences, avant-fusion and social satire may make your head spin at an accelerated rate. Actual brain damage is unlikely, in most cases." **John Shirley**

"*Codename Prague* is a thrill-a-minute combination of James Bond, Robert Ludlum, and cyberpunk set in a dangerous, erotic, and not-as-distant-as-you'd-wish future." **Mike Resnick**

Dr. Identity, or, Farewell to Plaquedemia

"D. Harlan Wilson's hilarious meta-pulp SF novel, *Dr. Identity*, is a funhouse mirror whose cartoonish distortions continually amaze and amuse—until one realizes that what we're seeing is a disturbingly accurate vision of ourselves. An instant avant-pop classic by a major new talent." **Larry McCaffery**

"Readers with a taste for wacky experimental fiction will enjoy D. Harlan Wilson's *Dr. Identity, or, Farewell to Plaquedemia*, a pulp science fiction novel set in the postcapitalist city of Bliptown." *Publishers Weekly*

"Madcap, macabre black comedy ... Wilson's sardonic, riotously imaginative vision of the future holds a mirror up to our own increasingly chaotic society and makes provocative entertainment." *Booklist*

"*Dr. Identity* is a rollicking romp through a future so absurd, it can't help but feel real. D. Harlan Wilson shows us everything we know—but wish we didn't—about ourselves." **Robert Venditti**

"This book's better'n the bushelful of Benzedrine-spiked donut holes with which Dr. Identity tries to bribe his students into civilized demeanor! Pomo cybertheory never tasted so good or made you fly this high!" *American Book Review*

Peckinpah: An Ultraviolent Romance

"A bludgeoning celluloid rush of language and ideas served from an action-painter's bucket of fluorescent spatter, *Peckinpah* is an incendiary gem and very probably the most extraordinary new novel you will read this year." **Alan Moore**

"Wilson's surreal view of a midwestern town called Dreamfield features the author's trademark prose which goes from violent to hysterical to bizarre—sometimes within the same sentence ... all the while leaving behind witty commentary and observances on the rural lifestyle." *Horror Fiction Review*

"*Peckinpah* ... proves that Wilson is either a genius or a madman, in all likelihood a crazed hybrid of both. A book that will delight Wilson's fans and mortally shock the uninitiated." **Eric Miles Williamson**

They Had Goat Heads

"Wilson delights in turning language to new and exciting uses." *Shroud Magazine*

"D. Harlan Wilson doesn't just gaze into the abyss. He dives headlong into it, pulling us with him and laughing maniacally all the way down." **Tim Waggoner**

"Funny, experimental, troubling, this brilliant collection of short stories proves conclusively that D. Harlan Wilson is a maverick author of genius." **Rhys Hughes**

Blankety Blank: A Memoir of Vulgaria

"Wilson has been duly anointed as speculative fiction's most unpredictable stylist." *Booklist*

"This comedy of menace, this spooky Kabuki, is never comfortable to inhabit but is as enjoyable as Krazy Kat just the same—the author indulges himself to the hilt and denies himself nothing." *Rain Taxi*

"The exquisite tilt of this novel runs us all off the board and on; its originality is a weapon. Firing at that bullseye on time." **Barry N. Malzberg**

"If you had a time machine and could secure the living brains of James Thurber and Andre Breton ripped untimely from their skulls, run them through a juicer, then mainline the blended liquid neurons, you might become a writer like D. Harlan Wilson ... If this be 'interstitial' fiction, then it's a case of the interstices expanding like a galaxy to overwhelm whatever bland shores once flanked them." **Paul Di Filippo**

Published by Raw Dog Screaming Press
Bowie, MD

First Edition

Cover image: Brett Weldele
Book design: Jennifer Barnes

Printed in the United States of America

ISBN 978-1-935738-29-9

Library of Congress Control Number: 2012954608

www.RawDogScreaming.com

other books by d. Harlan wilson

Novels

Codename Prague
Peckinpah: An Ultraviolent Romance
Dr. Identity, or, Farewell to Plaquedemia
Blankety Blank: A Memoir of Vulgaria

Criticism

Cultographies: They Live
Technologized Desire: Selfhood & the Body in Postcapitalist Science Fiction

Fiction Collections

They Had Goat Heads
Pseudo-City
Stranger on the Loose
The Kafka Effekt

"I am a superior being suffering from a nervous breakdown."
E. V. Odle, *The Clockwork Man*

For the Unnamable

table of contents

little more than an amphibious vacuum. Vacuums inhibit the status quo and cause psoriasis, among other trickledown effekts, but remember that dry skin is the primary accelerator of syncretism and xenophobia in some communities. Hand cream helps. I recommend Cetaphil, the sponsor of this multivalent broadcast and the source of my expansive and fecund livelihood. Thus spake **Travis Manderbean**. Let's take a few calls from our listeners. Hello this is **Travis Manderbean**. Hello. **Travis Manderbean** here. Hello. Hello there. Is anybody there? Let's not take any calls then. Let's return to the issue of extraterrestrial aliens. The skinny white fellas. They are not from another planet. They are thoroughbred earthlings. They're just terrifically old people. Old people who have lost all their hair. Old people who have grown tired of wearing clothes. Old people who don't eat much. Old people whose noses and ears and genitals have fallen off. Old people whose pupils have ruptured and leaked blackness onto the hoary whites of their eyeballs. Ergo your archetypal alien à la countless blockbuster movies centering on strained friendships and family dynamics. Why don't they have wrinkles? If you live long enough, wrinkles go away. Where do they get their spaceships? Their ray guns? Their penchant for human abduction, penetration and experimentation? Old people are smart. Old people are interested in things. They like to make things. Especially the ones that don't submit to pathology or abandon their mnemonic turbines...

The outréman didn't see the trap. Nor did his alterity goggles; the asterisks on the dashboard of the eyescreen remained pale and inert.

The clothesline caught him in the chest. Any higher and it might have beheaded him. His legs sprung out and up and he pinwheeled backwards while continuing to accelerate forwards. The driftdisc sputtered into the dirt and severed a cactus at the heel. Water gurgled onto the quiet earth.

He hit the ground like a sledgehammer. The blow would have killed most people, shattered their bones and exploded their organs.

He lost wind.

The body artists hid behind the gargantuan skeletons of whales and elephants and dinosaurs. They lurched into the sunlight and closed on their prey.

They exhibited fabulous deformities. The supposed leader appeared to be composed of plasticine clay and moved forward in stop-motion animation—awkward, disjointed, clumsily serpentine. One step behind him was a man in chimneysweep-chic sartorials with the brideshead of Dick Van Dyke.

The deformities of their entourage ranged from prosaic fins, gills, beaks, tails and other animalia to the hard technologies of weaponized limbs, growthscreens, and retrofarscaped bandwidths of secondskin. No way to tell if they had been induced by timecrashes or surgical enhancement. It didn't matter. Fashion and Artistry mimicked Folly with pathological resolve.

INFODUMP, OR, THY PILES

Nobody knew when the timecrashes began. Without temporal uniformity and constructedness, there can be no history—real or illusory. Origins had become ardent Speculative Fictions. Most of these SFs, however, postulated that the timecrashes were fallout from the Stick Figure War (2406-2416 AR) What aspects of the SFW produced timecrashes, on the other hand, was a subject of endless debate. Most SFers claimed they resulted from widespread pseudoscientific tampering with the spacetime continuum to create more effektive metaphysical superweapons, an epidemic that terminally lacerated the carcass of reality.

Others said timecrashes had been conjured out of thin air by the Stix themselves and the war had never come to an end; in fact, the war was monotonously palpable, and humans felt the burns and bruises of "defeat" on a daily basis, if only psychologically, as the SFW currently unfolded on the battlefield of the unconscious, sometimes the preconscious. But this position relied upon the capacity for dreams to expose the (simulated) nature of "truth," "reality," etc. And nobody had dreamed in years. Hence the argument presupposed an imagined diegesis in which representations of "reality" might shed light on "reality," an intricate representation (of) itself...A few extremist SFers argued that timecrashes had nothing to do with the war. Rather, they materialized because of a surplus of godlessness and nihilism in the collective (un)consciousness that spilled out of the mind-body consortium onto the physical landscape, perverting it. Whatever the case, while nobody knew how long they had been around, timecrashes were here to stay.

The outréman stood and steadied his breath. A breeze kicked up. Dust devils sped away from his boots in galactic spirals.

—Take off your scarf and show us your face, said the Dick Van Dyke, grinning like a chimp.

The outréman cocked his head. The body artists converged on him. He raised a slow hand...

...and removed his gloves. Then his headgear. Then his alterity goggles. Then a pair of gloveliners. Then his scarf—it took eight careful revolutions to unwrap it from his neck. Then he mimicked removing a pair of gloves, as if in a silent film. Then he removed his earbuds and stuffed them in a pocket. Then he unbuttoned his jacket. Rebuttoned it. Unbuttoned it halfway, then all the way, then busied himself with a racetrack of zippers on his chest and abdomen, all with the excruciating performativity of a seasoned showman...The body artists got antsy, but they didn't attack him. For once, they exercised communal patience. Soon he would be dead. Soon they would consume him. Aestheticize his flesh.

...The outréman didn't take off his mask. He placed arms akimbo and nodded in friendly affirmation. Such behavior, of course, would only exacerbate his antagonists' default aggression and mania. But absurdist bravado seemed like the appropriate response mechanism, at least according to the first wave of impulses that directed the flows of his desires. He always tried to obey the first wave.

—Take it off, said a man with a goiterscreen projecting from his neck. The goiterscreen expanded and contracted, as if breathing. Its obscene surface crackled with static.

—A dead channel, intoned the outréman. That static reeks of oblivion and tranquility.

—Take the mask off. Now.

—The mask is the doorway to the soul. The soul is the doorway to the future of an illusion.

—Do what you're told or I'll do it for you!

—I wouldn't do that if I were you.

The body artist marched forward and reached out and snatched the mask from the outréman's face. It came free easily.

And ate the body artist's hand. The trauma exploded his goiterscreen into acidic flecks of celluloid...

The mask convulsed in the dirt. It coughed up phlegm, bile and oil.

It scuttled away.

The outréman's physiognomic prowess besieged normative parameters and the body artists struggled to negotiate and process it. If compelled to describe him to a sketch artist, they wouldn't know where to begin, other than with the usual suspects: hair, eyes, nose, mouth, chin...

—That was an expensive pretense, the outréman said sadly.

Blood poured from the body artist's wrist. Blood poured from the flapped crater where the goiterscreen used to be.

Astounded, he fainted, twitched. Died.

The Dick Van Dyke emitted an insect scream. His cohorts reacted like snapdragons.

The outréman tended to his cuticles. Then:

—The world of men burns with the persistence of gratuitous idiocy, he announced, raising a pointed eyebrow. I fondle the Udders of Chaos. I eat veal in the shadow of the Tall Window. Gonna sermonize, me. Let me tell you a story. A myth. A legend. It begins with a man. It ends with a city. The space between these polarities is marked by the slash of an aluminum grin.

The body artists stroked their extensions and implants in raw agitation.

—Things went sour when they erased obesity from the genetic code of the human contraption, said the outréman. Nobody appreciated that people actually enjoyed being fat; the texture, the very sight of flab pleased the corpulent subject. They didn't stop there. They dissolved gender, rendering straight lines from curves, manufacturing flat stuff from protuberances. They turned everybody's pigment the same color and made certain that everybody grew at the same rate and achieved the same height. They handed out fake rubber noses. Eventually the only distinguishing feature on a "person" was a hairdo, the one permissible artifact of identity and self-fashioning. Body communism. It failed. They blew up the city.

The body artists blinked.

—What I just told you, the outréman continued, is a metaphor for the narrative I am about to reveal. This is how it begins. There was a man who could transform into a city. This is how it ends.

In a painful flash of understanding, the body artists realized what they were up against. Tentatively they paced backwards despite the futility of escape.

INFODUMP, OR, THY PILES

The mythology of the man→city persisted for centuries and suffered the diachronic backpain of evolution and metamorphosis. Curiously, the man→city had only existed for half a century, at least according to some eschatologists. Experts of course attributed this temporal anomaly to timecrashes, as they attributed every anomaly that they couldn't deprocess, temporal or atemporal. Certain variables in the mythology stayed constant. The man→city was an inadvertent mass murderer, for instance, killing thousands, on occasion millions, depending upon the outrézone, whenever he transformed from skin and bone into wood and metal and concrete. Additionally, prominent apparatchiks held him responsible for an acceleration in global warming, a phenomenon attributed to the rapid manner in which, throughout the course of his transformation, he forced a reinscription of space and atmosphere as the earth struggled to accommodate his sudden, unanticipated metropolitan bulk. He was also indicted for the quickening of the science fictionalization of the social and cultural register, something well underway before his investment in the reality studio, and yet something that undeniably belonged to him, as the emergent knowledge of his existence and the capabilities of the human body kindled virtual forest fires of scientific, epistemological, ontological and metaphysical creativity, exploration and application. The moral(ity) of this latter narrative was a topic of fiery defibrillation. At any rate, the man→city had long been a household name, feared, fetishized and fixated on with Kierkegaardian rigor, an affliction exacerbated by the fact that nobody knew what he looked like, since nobody had ever seen him and lived to tell the tale.

And if in fact the outréman was the man→city, the body artists couldn't discern his face, and if by some hypothetical miracle they were set free, they would have no tangible basis on which to describe him, other than he was a man, not exceedingly tall, not terribly short, with a nettled, sonorous voice, and with gestures the likes of reptiles, slow and deliberate, yet on the verge of lashing out.

A body artist in stop-motion animation gathered courage and told the outréman to lie down on the ground and put his hands behind his head.

—I am a spatial anthropology, he replied. Spatial anthropologies don't lie down on the ground. They rise into the clouds and shatter heaven's skylights.

—That's enough clever talk, clever talker, said the Dick Van Dyke. This is your last chance.

—Last chance. Last chance for what? What will you to do to me? Molest me? Murder me? Swallow my soul? You don't even know. You're simply enacting the motions. Dionysian motions. Entropic motions. You're enslaved by a narrative that you can't see. You're characters in a trashy pulp novel. It ticks and it tocks—you can't stop the lynched pendulum from swinging like a dogtongue. You can enter it from infinite orifices. You can go backwards and forwards. You can put a bookmark in it, pause it. But unless you understand it, it means nothing. And yet this narrative is God and Guide. I am not the author. There is no author. There is Cause. There is Effekt. I roost on the Precipice and perceive the geographies of Dogshit. Through the vehicle of my body, you will learn the meaning of ragged storytelling. I am the Podium on which you may stand tall and pose questions with lethal answers. Interrogation is contingent upon desire, you Unholy Fuckers. Crack open my person like an egg and my fuming essence will flow into the gutters and drown all of the impersonators. These are mere snippets of my plagiarized word horde. My word horde is fractal and true. But in the end it will ring false. Mind you, Gentlemen Cunts: the scope of my assholery knows no boundaries.

The monologue struck a mutual chord. Enmity overwhelmed fear...

—*Scheißekopf.*

The body artists blitzed the outréman. In the face of the Unknown and the Incomprehensible, violence and aggression are the only viable resorts.

They beat him to a proverbial and literal pulp. Sometimes they took turns; sometimes they did it all at once. He let them. He bled for them. Twice he told them they were doing "seminal work in the field."

His bruises pulsed, grew larger and uglier, turned deeper shades of purple, then black. Blood flowed from his wounds and made small, orderly puddles in the sand.

They beat him until they couldn't beat him anymore. Fatigued, the body artists slumped over, gasping for breath.

Red-rimmed clouds flared onto the sky like rashes.

The outréman stood...and the puddles of blood disappeared into his wounds...and the wounds disappeared...and the bruises faded, faded, faded... He cracked his neck. He grinned a Cartesian grin as his flesh acclimatized to the assault, reconfiguring itself, preparing itself.

The body artists lifted their arms and reached out for him, fingers trembling...

It was the 1000 1st time he turned into Kyoto.

the 1st time i turned into kyoto

CRITERION PROSE

Grocery carts squeaked and clattered and rumbled up and down the aisles...

The blueberries looked good today. He opened a carton and tasted one of them. Tasted all right. A little sour, but he liked them sour, and when he bit down on the berry, its juices burst onto his teeth and palate and tongue. Few berries burst with that sort of fanaticism.

"Ahem."

He peered over his shoulder. A nonsequitor *Schutz* with white lambchop sideburns flexed a filigreed jaw and said, "What're you doing?"

Inquisitive eyes darted left, right, left...

"Yeah. I'm talking to you. What do think you're doing?"

"Me?" he replied. "Nothing. I'm testing these berries."

"No," said the nonsequitor *Schutz*. "You're *buying* those berries. This isn't a free-for-all. This isn't the Garden of Eden. There are rules. Food costs money. Food goes into your mouth—food gets bought."

"I'm not buying flat berries."

"I've been watching you. We've all been watching you." The nonsequitor *Schutz* pointed at the ceiling and moved his finger in a broad, drowsy circle. "You have taste-tested nearly every fruit in the supermarket."

"You're exaggerating."

"There are bite marks in the pears. There are bite marks in the apples. There are bite marks in the kiwis."

He enacted a complex hesitation. "I didn't do that."

"You did that, sir."

"You have no evidence."

"We have obtained thousands of analogue and digital video recordings of your actions. These recordings are self-replicating and have been transmitted to thousands of local law enforcement agencies."

Beat. "I'm not buying flat berries," he repeated.

"You will buy them flat," the nonsequitor *Schutz* bleated. "You will buy them unflat."

He smiled. He nodded.

He ran away.

Derailed, the nonsequitor *Schutz* fell over, then took him out at the heels with a meaty forearm.

A fistful of blueberries sailed through the air in slow motion, froze at their peak, then fastforwarded into a sharp descent and exploded against the checkered tile floor…

They wrestled. Awkwardly. He was slim and in good shape but not very coordinated, and the nonsequitor *Schutz* was overweight and out of shape and extremely uncoordinated. They sort of rolled around on each other, failing to apply headlocks. Shoppers observed them with canned wonderment. Finally the nonsequitor *Schutz* managed to grab a bottle of balsamic vinegar and whack him in the head with it.

Things went dark.

He awoke in a stock room on his back. Giant anthrohydraulic forklifts moved wooden crates on and off shelves that rose to a distant ceiling. The floor shook as they loped across it with heavy iron steps. Rabbitear antennae extended and retracted from their braincubes as their eyes pulsed red and burned barcodes and brand names onto the crates.

He pushed himself up.

A forklift dropped a crate. It fell to the cement floor in fasttime, exploded in slow motion. Synthetic dirt and genetically enlarged legumes burst from the cracks.

The commotion excited the forklifts. They plodded haphazardly across the stock room, crashing into shelves, crashing into themselves, tripping over stacks and piles of detritus, collapsing…

Things went dark.

He awoke…somewhere else. Dim, musty. Cement floor, cold against the skin. But not the stock room. Realtime deceived him. It was not a dream…

Broad-shouldered stickmen shocked him with cattle prods and shouted about the inoculents. The features, the contours of their faces escaped his (in)sights...

...opened his flesh. He bled electric ants......dashed across the floor, mandibles clicking like spilled birdshot pellets...

Things went dark.

He awoke...somewhere else. A waiting room or lobby. Bright lights. Canary yellow walls. Cheap carpet. Tables fanned with homemaking magazines. Chairs...

Faint Cashmere Muzak crackled from a square speaker in the ceiling.

He was alone. He sat upright and gazed absently at the far wall. There was an ornately framed photograph hanging on it at a slight angle. The only photograph in the room...

...entered his screen of vision...ears and a mustache...bald...The man wore navy blue slacks and a short-sleeved dress shirt and a thin tie with thick stripes. "I am an Organizational Leadership Provider," said the man. "The acronym for this title is appropriately OLP. I have been trained as such since birth. Hence you may say that I am a born Organizational Leadership Provider—viz., a Born Leader." He brandished a pen and clipboard. "Call me Ishmael. L. Ron Ishmael." He tapped the plastic nametag on his shirt with the pen. "Please refer to me as Mr. Ishmael in professional conversation. Your name, please?"

"Where am I?" he uttered.

Mr. Ishmael said, "Name, please, sir?"

"I forgot." He leaned to one side and squinted at the photograph on the wall. It wasn't large, but he could see it clearly—too clearly, as if viewing it through a telescope. Or a microscope...It was a photograph of a city, captured from a remote crow's nest in the sky.

"You forgot." Mr. Ishmael recorded the information, intently, white-knuckled, fingers trembling, as if carving words into the clipboard. "Do you have amnesia?"

"I don't know. I don't know what I have." Beat. "Amnesia...Amnesia tempers the bashful rat like an unsuspecting skinhole." Beat. "I've never heard that maxim. I don't know what it means." Beat. "I don't know what I have."

Mr. Ishmael nodded perfunctorily. "I'm familiar with this affliction. For sake of record, I am going to call you, uh, Misterrrrrr"—running a finger down the clipboard—"uhhhhhhh, *Plissken*. As in *Snake* Plissken. Indeed, sir. That's what we'll call you. We always identify criminals by way of corny action heroes, even though we usually don't tell criminals about this practice. That's a secret among us Born Leaders. You are the spitting image of Kurt Russell, if I might add, except for the hair and the face and the body. You are certainly a Caucasian. You are a man, I think."

"I'm not a criminal," said Plissken.

"As you wish." Smiling, Mr. Ishmael discussed the nature of Being-in-Charge and his primal *Dasein*. "First of all, one must set a good example. Additionally, one must act accordingly. Then one must understand the laws of social Darwinism, logical systems, sensoria and noumenons. And one must hold one's chin up when one upholds the policies of the supermarket. Yes, one must be brave, thrifty, reverent…"

Rapt, Plissken tried to figure out what city was depicted in the photograph. It occurred to him that it might not be a photograph, but a portrait, or perhaps a photograph that had been airbrushed or doktored to resemble a portrait…Something about the sky. It looked rusted. Corroded.

Virile.

Lush mountains embraced the city. Enormous Asian symbols punctuated the green peaks; trees had been mindfully cut down in their intricate shapes. One of the symbols burst aflame…

Difficult to perceive the buildings. He noted a unique architectural variety. He wanted a closer look.

Patellas rotated like combination locks…Knees retracted into ligaments, enabling the levers of thighs…

L. Ron Ishmael checked his soliloquy and put a hand on Plissken's shoulder. "If you please, sir. You are under arrest."

"Arrest? For what?" He sat, limply, as if the OLP's touch had wounded him.

Mr. Ishmael placed the clipboard against his chest and crossed his arms over it. He looked down at Plissken disappointedly. "Empty rhetoric.

Disposable prose. There's nothing worse. Well. The thing is, you attempted to steal the supermarket. You aimed a gun at the supermarket's Grand Dragon of the Realm and told him to give it to you. He said, quote, 'What?' You said, quote, 'Give me the goddamned supermarket.' It's right here." He showed him the clipboard. "It's written down right here. Expletive and all."

"I didn't do that."

"The question concerning how you would go about confiscating the supermarket remains problematic. Insidious logistics. A supermarket is a rather large apparatus, after all, and you, we've concluded, are just a man. How would you unearth the apparatus? How would you carry it away? Where would you hide it? And what would you do with the employees? A supermarket is not a supermarket without its technological extensions. Otherwise it is merely a receptacle of goods. A box of boxes."

Beat.

"As I was saying," Mr. Ishmael continued, "once you have been processed by the supermarket's Grand Titan of the Dominion and his squadron of Furies, you will be turned over to the local authorities. I am in no position to make a judgment as to what they will do with you. They may let you go. They may put you under arrest and process you in a fashion that resembles the very manner in which you have been processed by the Born Leaders of the supermarket. Then again, they may..."

His voice floated away, far, far away, across the static vastness, through the tall reeds of savannahs, on a bed of oysterflesh...Plissken succumbed to a weird hypnosis...**Novocain...Butane...Metropocalypse**...The city entranced him. Commanded him. He had no excuse. The city defied his memory, his identity...Was it Tokyo? Hong Kong? Shanghai?...No. A Japanese city. He knew virtually nothing about Asian architecture and landscapes other than what Godzilla and Bruce Lee films had revealed to him. But he sensed a yawning Japanese character.

The photograph engulfed the wall.

No. The city leaked out of the frame and engulfed the wall...Plissken shuddered as it expanded, showing him street grids...clusters of buildings...

colorful gardens and bursts of evergreen…wingtip rooftops and skyblue rivers and great gold-plated Buddhas…

Eyes glazed, Plissken exclaimed, "I feel sick!" Then, quieter, in an almost indecipherable murmur: "I don't feel good."

Mr. Ishmael bowed his head. "I'm sorry to hear this. But your health is your own affair as long as it doesn't affect the health of others in some fashion. Then your health becomes my concern. Then your health becomes everybody's concern. I'm going to write that down."

Plissken produced an obscene burp and vomited in the chair beside him. It was mercury.

"Foul, Mr. Plissken." Mr. Ishmael stared at the quicksilver discharge like a flower of evil. "Are you going to do that again? The real Snake Plissken wouldn't do that. Mr. Kurt Russell wouldn't do that. I've met Mr. Russell, incidentally. We had dinner once in London in a private room in the back of an upscale restaurant. The name of the restaurant escapes me. My sister went to school with the actor's daughter. It was a hell of a time. Mr. Russell paid for everything and I got drunk and met a girl. Nothing happened, but it might have been the best night of my life."

Plissken doubled over, groaning. He fell forward off the chair like a crash-test dummy. Mr. Ishmael stepped aside and allowed him to collapse. "I hope this isn't some feeble attempt to deceive me," he said. "I'm no stranger to the deception of everymen."

A fever swelled from his core. Sweat rolled from gaping pores. The shivers… Hot flashes hit him like snapkicks. Cottonmouth…

The city spread across the walls, the ceiling. He tried not to look at it. To close his eyes…But they wouldn't close, and the city expanded, spires and irimoyas and pagodas reaching for him, eating space like freezerfrost.

Shadows ran down Mr. Ishmael's body as the flickering city gained momentum. "I saw a television show when I was a child that changed my life," he remarked. The tone of his voice had changed. He spoke in a vague trance. "A husband and wife and child entered a store that sold planets. A salesman ushered them down a long aisle, underscoring the positive aspects of each piece of merchandise. Eventually the child got bored and wandered off. There was a small black box on a low shelf. The child picked it up and studied it, turning it over and over with tiny hands. The salesman realized what was happening and he and the husband and wife shouted for the child not to open the box. But the child opened the box. It contained a black hole, and the black hole sucked the television show into it, and the screen went black, and it stayed black. The television never worked again. This was the moment I became conscious of death. Part of me died in this moment. One day the rest of me will die. I'm waiting."

Plissken's throat closed. Veins inflated on his neck.

Mnemonic strobes. Unspeakable pain. Nightclash of ignorant armies…

The city's fingers closed into a gunmetal fist.

Explosion of sound and light. Existential screech. Then: a Zero Degree of Meaning………Image of a mushroom cloud over Hiroshima. It rose into the sky in slow motion, in fasttime, in realtime. In monochrome…

…and the city pixilated, imploding into beige vapor…

With a powerful gasp of air, Plissken's eyes sprung open. Froze open…

Adrenalized, he climbed into a chair, heartbeat thumping in his ears.

His vision wavered. He made obscene faces as he struggled to focus…

Eternity dissolved into clarity.

There was no picture on the wall. It had disappeared.

He vomited again. It was soil.

"Mr. Plissken," said Mr. Ishmael…

"I'm sorry," he croaked. "I didn't mean to do it. Nobody means to throw up."

"What about bulimics? Their throwup is purposeful and deliberate. One often makes oneself throw up in the grasp of a hangover as well. One often feels better that way."

"I…I…I can't…"

"What is that?"

"…I…"

"That bruise on your arm. There." Mr. Ishmael gesticulated. "It's getting bigger. Do you see it?"

Plissken lifted his arm and stared at it in horror. A shade of sick, alien purple oozed across the skin.

"Where's the telephone?" said Mr. Ishmael, making no effort to look for a telephone.

"It hurts," said Plissken matter-of-factly.

Seconds later, the bruise had spread across his entire body. His skin hardened, darkened, cracked…He withered like a stick of vellum on fire, shoulders coming together, fracturing into infinite shards…

…I…

A tower burst from Plissken's chest—the keen Japanese observer might recognize it as the Kyoto Tower, the tallest structure in the city, with its long white spire, orange observation deck and black antenna—and impaled L. Ron Ishmael. Dazzling flames of gore spewed from his eyes, nose, ears and mouth. As the tower forged a tumescent path, it tore him apart like a bag of oilpaint…

It was the first time he turned into Kyoto.

☰

before the 1st time i turned into kyoto
PHOTOGRAPH

三

before the 1st time i turned into kyoto
CRITERION PROSE

INFODUMP, OR, THY PILES

When the "I" was five, they plagiarized an alien invasion from Isaak Asimov's novel *To Unearth the Bruises Underground*, trying to pass it off as the Genuine Article. The aliens resembled Asimov insofar as they possessed fins on their cheeks that, looked at askance, might be mistaken for the memorable science fiction author's egregious sideburns. Hence the meta-element of the invasion, *realpolitik* critics later brought to the attention of the eager and hungry public.

"Isaak Asimov is attacking us." According to an amateur mockumentary of the event shot in Technicolor with a 16mm spring-wound camera, several onlookers uttered these words as they witnessed the *étrangers qui sont faux* fall from the Texas sky, propelled downward by the fibrous pterodactylic wings of souped-up fangliders.

Wielding glitzy pulp scifi ectoblasters, they destroyed millions of humans and ravaged the social, physical, and telefissional landscape. Bodies spasmed into impossible poultice, disintegrated into superfine dust. Houses and stripmalls and skyscrapers collapsed. Trees were stripped of their bark and hung out to dry. Mindscreens shot up in price, becoming hopelessly unaffordable to the mass of manchildren...It would have gone on and on until nothing but covergirls and vintage auteurs remained, but as with all alien invasions, authentic or staged, eventually a virus whitewashed the aberration. In this instance, the virus resulted from overexposure to WD-40, which the aliens used to grease their intricate joints, but the hydrocarbon spray possessed an inert ingredient that maligned synthetic intestines, giving the aliens accelerated cases of colon cancer. They shriveled and died as quickly and whimsically as their attack had been plagiarized.

The authors of what came to be known as "War of the Worlds IV: The Irreality Show" were not apprehended until twenty years later, on the twenty-sixth birthday of "I," which "I" spent alone, with a bottle of illegal Russian vodka and enough low-grade hemp to knit an afghan, watching reruns of *The Jeffersons* on Nick at Nite. They interrupted the show to inform viewers about the bust. George Jefferson morphed into the President of the United States of Amerika, who explained that the perpetrators of "The Irreality Show" — [shotgun imaginarium of two half-naked teenagers in a red room screaming as grizzled men in blowtorch masks persecute them] — had no real impetus for siccing a "rock brigade" [ref. Def Leppard's *On through the Night*] of Asimovian extraterrestrial simulacra on the human race with the arachnoid mercilessness of Wellsian Martian terrorists. They were simply young, uninformed and naïve. [Repeat torture image. Repeat again. Insert outtake of Ronald Reagan in *Bedtime for Bonzo*, then a State of the Union address.] "We can't blame young people for their actions," concluded the President. "But we can certainly hold the honkies accountable and punish them for their actions. Ducks pathologize their ducklings — end of story. Goodnight."

Abrupt cut back to *The Jeffersons* in which George, the treacherously bitter patriarch, dishes out a racist invective to his son Lionel for fraternizing with a white girl...

He turned off the mindscreen, opened amniotic curtains, and looked out the window.

Crooked highrises climbed into the vermillion sky like scoliotic antiquarians. Even the smokestacks and antennas were kinked.

INFODUMP, OR, THY PILES

In the wake of the "The Irreality Show," people forgot how to make things. The aliens destroyed most major cities, all of which were refurbished, to varying degrees, and yet almost every new city contained sectors that appeared to have been constructed by the Uncoordinated, the Disabled, the Inchoate and the Incompetent. At the same time, an unidentifiable aura of purpose, orderliness and design marked the deformed cityscapes, especially when observed from afar, like crop circles.

He blinked. He fingered his eye.

INFODUMP, OR, THY PILES

To reclaim the last twenty years of "I"...A mediatized blur. Too much screentime had infringed on subjective reality. After "I"'s parents died in the Crash, orphanages staged a brief comeback, foster care being outlawed as too broad and encouraging a forum for couples to unleash libidinal aggression. Municipal Urchin's Annex was a fully technologized outfit that combined medieval and postfuturist aesthetics, with an emphasis on the latter, and except for the Patriarch-in-Chief, who nobody ever saw, the place was entirely run by outmoded, over-the-hill robosapiens that constantly broke down and had to be replaced, sometimes by altogether non-sentient organisms.

Nonetheless "I" didn't remember anything outrageously traumatic, even when "I" reviewed/revised footage shot from geostationary orbit. This was not the domain of Oliver Twist. Porridge flowed in abundance, for instance, dished out freely even if an orphan didn't ask for it in a polite monotone. Furthermore, orphans were permitted and even encouraged to watch television *in extremis*, and the Annex enjoyed government-subsidized mindscreens in every room, including toilets and select walk-in closets, the government justifying such endowments for reasons of sheer pity—"They're goddamn orphans, for Chrissakes!" the city commissioner squealed whenever the matter surfaced in roundtable discussions—which nobody could argue with for more than a few seconds at risk of being lethally branded for antiempathic conduct.

A Smaug Turbo GT landed on a nearby rooftop. Wings folding back with a hydraulic whistle, the vehicle crouched on its hind legs, and a staircase opened and descended from the abdomen...Steam hissed from eyes, jaw, ears. At least twenty Asian men in black business suits and hibiscus tribal masks filed down the staircase, strode to the edge of the rooftop, and stepped off.

The Smaug's stomach swallowed the staircase and its eyes flared back to life. As it opened its wings and prepared for liftoff, the rooftop gave, and it vanished in a soft geyser of rubble and dust.

He waited for the building to collapse with bated breath. It didn't happen. Depressed, he closed the curtains and returned to the mindscreen.

INFODUMP, OR, THY PILES

Ultimately the poor reconstruction of cities didn't matter. By the time "I" accomplished the age of thirty, the Stick Figure

War was well underway. And then came the timecrashes, and the zoneshifts, and the ominous volatility of reality and spacetime. Chaos became the rule, schizophrenia a normative condition, pathology the Middle C on the keyboard of existence. Life as a shithouse Rottweiler. The riptide of the human condition and its natural and constructed landscapes and noospheres slipped backwards and forwards in time with weird and relentless rigor. History fell into oblivion.

四

the 2nd time i turned into kyoto
CRITERION PROSE

"Good morning, 'Sam.' Nice to see you again." Arm extended, Dr. Grindhaüß strode across the stained, spring-loaded mat.

"Sam" shook his hand. "Is that my name? 'Sam'? I forgot. What's my last name?"

Dr. Grindhaüß adjusted the collar of his gee. "Beats me. But surnames are superfluous. *Überflüssig.* As you know."

"Actually they're quite useful," said "Sam." "How else can we tell one 'Sam' from another?"

Pitiable smile. "By creases in the palms," replied the doktor. "Nobody's creases are the same." He admired his palms, noting the deep lifelines curled around the thumbplates, then slowly drew hands into fists. He took three paces backwards, said, "Bow," and snapped into position.

"Sam" followed suit.

"Hajime!"

The routine: spar for twenty minutes, give or take, all of which "Sam" is billed for, of course, but Dr. Grindhaüß insists that a good, prolonged fight before a session "aids and abets" "Sam"'s treatment and will eventually lead to a much speedier recovery from the various neuroses and pathologies that harrow him. If nothing else, it produces healthy endorphin "windsprints" that allow "Sam" to articulate himself with greater precision and enthusiasm during the session. Additionally, in the doktor's words, "Physical confrontation will help to assuage the verbal and psychological confrontation that I will forthwith exert and mediate."

"Sam" didn't mind. He liked to fight, and he had consistently improved since he began taking lessons three years ago at the doktor's behest. It used to be that Dr. Grindhaüß kicked his ass up and down the mat. Now he only kicked it one way or the other.

The spar always ended with a knockout effekted by way of some elaborate, technologized blow. Today the doktor employed an old-fashioned *ozuki* kick.

To revive the patient, he punched him in the heel with maximum leverage.

A powerfully built man, the doktor looked awry and unnatural, mainly as a result of unremitting cosmetic surgeries to negate wrinkles and enhance musculature, but the primary catalyst was his lack of hair, anywhere, face, arms, chest, legs, groin—he had shown "Sam" on multiple occasions—which Dr. Grindhaüß claimed to be a perfectly natural phenomenon, something he had been born with, or rather without, a prenatal affair in any event. Consequently his skin exhibited a rubbery texture, as if he had been shrinkwrapped in latex, with the exception of his scalp, the only fertile ground on his body. His slicked-back onyx hair appeared painted onto the head, but he insisted on its veracity, and he had even encouraged "Sam" to yank on it during moments of grave doubt. On one occasion he allowed "Sam" to administer a lie detector test to determine the authenticity of the hair once and for all. The doktor passed without incident, the needles of the polygraph inking virtual flatlines across an unraveling roll of papyrus. "Sam" continued to be skeptical. But he appreciated his therapist's efforts to make him feel comfortable and worthy of an opinion.

"Domo arigato." Dr. Grindhaüß helped "Sam" to his feet.

"Domo arigato," "Sam" repeated, massaging his heel. Dr. Grindhaüß hoisted him over a shoulder, carried him into a small locker room, and laid him out on a massage table. He applied a diluted liniment to the heel, rubbing it in with care.

They removed their gees. They showered. There was only one stall and they had to trade off standing in front of the nozzle. They shared a bar of soap. They shared a towel. Finally they put their normal clothes on—blue Nehru suit and bolo tie for the doktor, brown leisure suit and plain necktie for "Sam"—and took their respective positions in an armchair and chaise lounge.

"Can I sit in the Big Chair today?" asked "Sam."

"Certainly."

They switched.

The doktor closed his eyes and fell asleep.

"Sam" implored him to wake up. He didn't. "Sam" shook him. Dr. Grindhaüß hugged his knees, eyeballs like metronomes behind the lids. "Sam" got frantic.

The doktor's eyes popped open. "I forgot—I can't sit on this damned thing. Damned thing is too comfortable. God damn this comfy chair."

They switched again.

Beeswax from a burning votive candle dribbled onto a cherrywood mantle. The flame was small and loud.

"Sam" said, "I turned into a city yesterday."

"Go on."

"It might have been a dream. It was probably a dream. I know this."

"That's impossible," Dr. Grindhaüß rebuked. "Human beings no longer have dreams. Fallout. *Sinnesfäule*. The last documented dream was decades ago. It doesn't happen. It can't happen. You know this."

"Right…Right. I know this…Are you real?"

"As real as you want me to be. Tell me more about the city. Your metamorphosis. It stinks of the abject."

"Sam" told him the story, beginning with his arrest. He talked at length about the minutia of the city. Repeatedly he used the word "sharp" in reference to rooftops and dark places. Dr. Grindhaüß didn't interrupt him. He observed him indolently, nodding and cocking his head during moments of swollen exposition.

"You were arrested?" he asked, exercising his fingers.

"I don't know," said "Sam." "Maybe. Like I said, it's all kind of fuzzy. Picture perfect, too. I remember it like it was yesterday."

"Didn't this happen yesterday?"

"Yes. Hence my sharp memory of the incident. And yet the incident remains murky. Inscrutable."

"You mentioned the word 'sharp' again?"

"What?"

"*Sharp*. You've said that word at least fifty times today." He removed his spectacles and began to clean them with a silk handkerchief.

"I have? Does that mean something?"

He removed his coat and rolled up his sleeve to the armpit and began to flex his bicep. "Look at this fucker," said the doktor. "Astonishing vascularity. I'm a fiftysomething-year-old man, by God." It was true. Veins encrusted the hard ball of flesh that burst from his arm like ripe fruit. As he cranked his forearm up and down, up and down, the veins pulsed in a wriggling symphony.

"If I was a heroin addict I'd be set for life." He rolled down the shirtsleeve and buttoned it. "All right. Time's up. See you next week."

"I just got here."

"Yes. You were saying something about...sharpnesses? Yes. The word 'sharp.' You keep reiterating it. This is because you have a small penis and it's all you can think about. Nothing shines more light across the hills and vales of your consciousness like the galactic signpost of your diminutive inadequacy. 'Sharp' denotes something that is pointed, like a pencil, or a harpoon, or a flagpole. Some flagpoles have bulbous tips. Nevertheless. A pointed thing is a long thing, or in any case an extended thing, unlike that thing between your legs. You want to be 'sharp,' in other words, which is to say, you want a bigger cock."

"I don't have a small penis," "Sam" admitted. "Actually it's rather large. Formidable, I'd argue. You just saw it in the shower. You were staring right at it. Your eyes were wide. You looked like a manga character. You looked scared."

Dr. Grindhaüß frowned at his patient's crotch. "Ah yes. I remember now." He stood and stepped behind his chair, monitoring the votive. "Tell me more about your transformation."

"I've told you everything."

"Tell me more."

"Do you want me to make something up?"

"No need to bite my head off. I'm trying to help you."

"Sam" blinked at the ceiling. Dr. Grindhaüß sat back down in the chair and inspected the paisley swirls on his tie.

"Sam" said, "My memory isn't working properly."

"Oh."

"I have difficulty remembering certain things. For example, I don't remember the Stick Figure War. Was that during my lifetime? Honestly I can't remember."

"Curious."

"Timecrashes wiped out everybody's memory. I think mine is especially wiped out. I don't even think it's mine."

The doktor coughed, once. "*Especially* wiped out. You think you're special, then."

"I didn't say that."

"You said 'especially.'"

"Yeah, but I didn't mean it like that."

"Like what?"

"Meaning isn't fixed. It's fluid. You told me that. You always tell me that. Verbatim."

"And yet you say 'I didn't mean it like that.' Meaning you meant it another way, a very specific way. A special way."

"No."

"And if something is wiped out, it's wiped out. There are no degrees. Something cannot be 'especially' wiped out just as something cannot be 'especially' human. Or inhuman. Or dead."

"There are degrees of inhumanity."

The votive went out. Dr. Grindhaüß lit another one. "Timecrashes are unfortunate incongruities," he said. "Different subjects experience them in different ways."

"I understand."

"No you don't. Nobody understands anything. That's the problem. Timecrashes have negated objectivity. The objective world has ceased to exist."

"I thought you always said objectivity was a myth."

"Hmm." Gripping his elbows, Dr. Grindhaüß strode across the office and gazed out a tall, narrow sash window.

"I did a little research," said "Sam," "and I think I know what city I turned into. It was Kyoto. The symbols in the mountains. No other city in Japan has symbols quite like that."

"No other city in Japan has symbols quite like that," echoed the doktor.

"Yes. But that's not it. I mean, the research I did—it didn't matter. I know it was Kyoto anyway. I don't know how I know. I don't know why. I've never been to Kyoto. I've never thought about Kyoto. I may have never even spoken the word Kyoto, ever, in my life, until today. And yet…Why didn't I turn into Toledo? Or Montreal? I've been to those cities. I still think it was a dream. I know dreams are impossible. I know over half of the homeless population in the world consists of former oneirologists."

"Now you are reiterating the word 'know.' You know this, you don't know that. Ergo your epistemological dilemma vis-à-vis the monstrous-masculine desire."

"Sam" turned onto his side. "Monstrous-masculine?"

"Indeed." Dr. Grindhaüß stepped away from the window and made an anxious waving motion that "Sam" perceived as a motion he would make if a monster were attacking him. "I won't bore you with the gory details. Well, perhaps a touch of gore." He lit a cigarette, smoked it, and put it out in the bowl of a gold hookah. "Essentially the monstrous-masculine—viz., the *quote* male monster *unquote*, a decentered ape-creature projected onto the abjected protagonist that is your Self—this evil motherfucker connotes a fear of castration and facilitates an Oedipal conflict with regards to other people *slash* characters on the *quote* hangnail's edge *unquote* of the social field into which you have been interpellated. Ergo, for the man to become the monster, whatever form it takes, thusly"—he lifted his hands and knotted them into claws and made a twisted face—"or thusly"—his face went blank, his limbs rigid—"whatever the form, he negotiates and to some degree annihilates feelings of rabid disempowerment."

"Can something be annihilated to a small degree?" "Sam" interrupted. "Isn't annihilation a non-negotiable...I don't know. You get annihilated, or you annihilate something—that's it, right? You can't partially annihilate something or get partially annihilated. Just like you can't be partially human. Or inhuman. Or dead."

Dr. Grindhaüß eyeballed "Sam," said, "You said 'annihilate' six times and 'something' three times," then continued. "Your alleged transformation into the *quote* monster *unquote* belongs to the realm of the fantastic, i.e., fantasy. In short, your condition, your affliction, your delusion, viz., this horseshit about transforming into a city, which we might call *metromorphia*...hmm"—he wrote the word down in a cordovan leatherbound journal—"this instance of metromorphia dictates three primary ephemera. One, as stated, an anxiety about disempowerment. Two, the activation of your death drive as a means of not wanting to be abject any longer. And three, an inevitable psychic bewilderment apropos the Jekyll *slash* Hyde binary created by the monstrous-masculine versus you, the everyman, the ordinary guy, the nothing, the superzero. You are a superzero. In the end, we are all superzeros. Everybody lives and dies and is forgotten. That's why we feel bad. That's why we turn into monsters. It makes us feel…good." He laughed to indicate what one does when one feels good.

"I feel sick," said "Sam."

"Perhaps some music, then." Dr. Grindhaüß sat at his desk and touched a knob on a vintage Crossley radio that looked like a Catholic church. The sound of Jim Nabors singing "Ave Maria" crackled from the speakers. "I like this asshole's voice," he said. "Who would've thought Gomer Pyle could carry a tune? And such a deep and powerful tune. You probably don't know who Gomer Pyle is. Long before your time. Mine, too."

"Sam" vomited hot celluloid onto the chaise.

Dr. Grindhaüß sprung to his feet. "Jesus Christ, 'Samuel'! That's an antique! At least throw up in a barf bag." He pointed at the dispenser near the foot of the chaise.

"This is what happened the first time," he said, strands of thermoplastic drooling from a half-open gash. "Only there was that picture. Now the picture's gone. Now it's inside of me."

The doktor retrieved a towel from an armoire, told "Sam" to get up, knelt and scrubbed the mess. "God almighty. What did you eat for breakfast? What is this business?"

"It's happening again. I'm going to change. I'm going to turn into Kyoto. I can feel the architecture welling up in me."

"Could you get me a can of Spot Shot? It's in the armoire."

A ringing noise pierced his brain like a javelin. Terrific anguish. "Help me," he whispered. "I'm…becoming…"

"Yes, yes," sighed Dr. Grindhaüß, scrubbing harder. "The dawn of the becoming-animal. The abstract machine must make the territorial assemblage open onto something else. Basic schizoanalysis. Unleash and embrace yourself in its true form. Do it. And then fetch me that Spot Shot. Our time is up anyway. You know what? Why don't we plan on…"

It was the second time he turned into Kyoto.

五

the 3rd time i turned into kyoto
PHONOGRAPH RECORDING

The voice radiates from a dark and spiritual chokeflow, flames of static enveloping its delicate articulations:

"A hollow breeze passes across the rooftops. Windmills spin and creak. Electricity flits up and down antennas. Three shingles loosen and blow into space...

"The city is empty.

"The city is alive. And decidedly gendered.

"He can feel the ducts and tunnels and sewerpipes of his underworld, the leaves of his kaiyushiki teien and konshoniwa gardens, and the cascades of his ryumon-no-taki waterfalls, his streets and temples and statues and matenrou of the distant past and the near future, his lights, the furious voltage of his lights, and the stench of stir-fry he disseminates from every wooden and paper and straw and asphalt and plaster and clay orifice...

"Leaning spires. Wrenched copestones. Bamboo...

"He senses everything, from the tallest, sharpest, most polyphonous and cumbersome edifice to the smallest shot glasses arranged in neat rows over mirrored sushi bars...

"He tries to move. To flex a muscle. Nothing. Stasis. Altogether immobile, helpless. A sitting duck. A smiling Buddha.

"He imagines the scream of a *daikaiju*...Dark, metallic, unending—the scream careens across space and time, vaporizing everything in its path.

"Urban psychosis. Metromorphic lunacy...It spans two minutes, or 200,000 years. Then, an earthquake...orange lightning bolts stretch across the body of Kyoto in a tectonic frenzy...

"For a moment he perceives himself as the shadow of a man-thing. A giant, lumbering humanoid with no face, no hair. His head scrapes against an orange ceiling of sky. Solar flares burst from his shoulders and thighs as he trudges across the city, feeble, aimless, alone...

"He awakes. Naked.

"The earth feels warm. Cooked.

"He discovers himself afoot, staring across a vast desert. No hills. No plant life. In every direction, a ravaged landscape—scorched and ruined. Dead.

"Hunger...

"His body temperature approaches a precarious index.

"He falls to his knees. Tears pool in the sand. Tears evaporate into the atmosphere.

"Many miles away, somewhere in the decayed folds of history, a man makes love to a prostitute. The narrative of their intercourse resounds with fuckwords and taboo mantras intersected by theoretical soliloquies on genetic operas. Their prose mitigates new flights of fancy as juices drip from the pages and entire paragraphs implode into mere splotches of pubic hair. Under threat of orgasm, the man grows violent. He resents the prostitute for conjuring his rich substance. He beats her lightly at first, tapping her face, scolding her breasts, but the onset of ejaculation sees his authorship move into the danger zone. Using a utility knife, he peels the vellum from her flesh and reveals the squalid pulp fantasies of her core...

"He awakens. He vomits...

"It is the third time he turns into Kyoto."

the 10th time I turned into Kyoto

STAGEPLAY

Certain Private Conversations in Two Acts and a Requiem

THE CHARACTERS

ARTHUR MILLER	TIMECRASH	DR. JOSEF MENGELE
ACTOR	ZONESHIFT	MIKLOS NYISZLI
THE MAN/LOMAN	POLISH JEW	

The action takes place in ARTHUR MILLER's private theater and dressing room and in various places the playwright visits in dreams and the Netherlands' red light district that elude the audience. A man in a satyr suit plays a melody on a flute — nobody can see him. The melody reminds listeners of high cliffs and treacherous geometry equations...ARTHUR is directing the play. He has arranged all of the actors on the ceiling. They stand upside-down. So does ARTHUR. He shoots footage with a 35mm camera so that everybody looks rightside-up, except their hair is on-end, and the skin of the fatter actors' faces has bunched up at the eyes and forehead. Clothing has been taped to the actors' bodies so that shirts, skirts, etc. don't hang in the wrong direction. Furniture, lamps, coat racks, etc. have been nailed to the ceiling in order to ensure verisimilitude.

An ACTOR unexpectedly falls from the ceiling onto the stage, cracking a strip of shellacked hardwood.

ACTOR   [*with urgency*]   I fell down.

ARTHUR Shit. I forgot about gravity.

[*At the cue, everybody else falls onto the stage...The actors get up and go outside for a smoke. One of them has broken his leg. Before lighting up, his peers throw him into a dumpster, as a gag...ARTHUR stares at the ceiling and wonders what to do. He can't seem to remember how everybody got up there in the first place...From the shadows a man walks onto the stage. He looks lost. ARTHUR doesn't notice him until he is almost within reach. He assumes the man is the new lighting director.*]

ARTHUR [*frowning*] Hello. What's your name again? The
        contractor told me, but I forget.

[*The man shakes his head, then shouts out the first name that comes to mind. It is garbled by a sinister roar of furnaces. He wears a brown leisure suit with a tight vest and wide plaid collar. Orange-tinted navigator sunglasses concomitantly deflect and reflect our attention. He's thin, not quite scrawny, and his limbs are too long.*]

THE MAN [*confused*] This is the wrong place.

ARTHUR [*uninterested*] I'll just call you Loman. As in *Low
        Man*. Get it? That's what I call everybody.

LOMAN   I'm supposed to be...somewhere else. I don't know
        where. Not here.

ARTHUR [*glancing up*] We're all supposed to be somewhere

else, Loman. Could you tweak the lights for me? That floodlight in particular. I'm trying to figure out how to get back on the ceiling. A change in lighting may be just what the doktor ordered.

[*A TIMECRASH shatters the wine glass of reality – unexpected, uninhibited, it rumbles across the stage. ARTHUR and LOMAN stare at its dark, mirrored, undulating bulk like an automobile collision they pass on the roadside. ARTHUR isn't sure what to make of it; he perceives the TIMECRASH with an expression that denotes utter familiarity and gruesome mystification. LOMAN, on the other hand, regards it with enmity, narrowing eyes and tightening lips...The TIMECRASH hits them like a cellophane avalanche...They freeze. Flesh dissolves into static and static peels off bones in long, digital filaments. ARTHUR's mouth vaporizes and a scream rolls out of the residual hole, a scream that gains impetus, rises in intensity until it breaks apart, splinters into interminable flats and sharps that quietly flow away, like flower petals in a river...The walls and the ceiling fade out...The stage ruptures, implodes...LOMAN is a DARKMAN now. No features, no color — only a razorsharp shadow. He falls into a spiraling void, the silhouette of JIMMY STEWART in Hitchcock's* Vertigo......*Silence. Blackness. A voice...*]

VOICE [of DENNIS HOPPER in *Blue Velvet*]   Now it's dark.

[*LOMAN awakes. Everything is different — clothes, time of day, ambiance, emotional bandwidth. No clouds in the sky. He monitors the sun and surmises it is about 3 p.m. He wears a confederate military uniform: slouch hat, butternut shell jacket and trousers, and square-toed brogans. Gripping the shaft of a musket, he feels euphoric, not angry and confused. But his joints ache...The sky momentarily flickers as a flock of ospreys passes across the spooled face of the sun... The birds' wings, heads and legs retract into their torsos and they morph into cannonballs. LOMAN realizes where he is...A clearing in the forest. Grassy. Smoky. Fricasseed...A battlefield...The cannonballs land on a cluster of trees. Soldiers with giant, unkempt mustaches explode from the smoke as if bounced off of springboards. More soldiers stumble out of the smoke and progress forward like zombies, spurting blood and vitals from blown-off limbs and jawbones...Despite the spectacle of gore, LOMAN continues to feel adequate. Not euphoric. Not happy. But not unhappy. And not afraid for his life. Fear of death triggers the metromorphia like no other catalyst...Somebody fires at LOMAN. Slugs whistle past his ears, riddle the soil with soft pops. He raises the musket, aims it at nobody in particular, and pulls the trigger. Misfire. Flaming gunpowder sprays his face and he flies backwards and somersaults and rolls into a tangled sitting position, dazed, ulcerated, legs splayed into a warped V... Through clouded vision, he watches another TIMECRASH surge out of the trees, devouring the dead and the half-dead... Usually TIMECRASHES don't occur so close together. Never, in fact...It collides with him. Turns him into swill. This time he hears thousands of voices, a pastiche of uxorious tongues and tantrics and ape-screeches...It's always different. Every time is a new time.]*

INFODUMP, OR, THY PILES

The mystery regarding the origin of time-crashes is further problematized by the frequent concurrence of zoneshifts, which ferry demolecularized bodies to different landscapes, sometimes to different planets, although never outside of the solar system, and usually to Venus, where the bodies molarize and burn into flickering emulsions. But off-world zoneshifts are rare.

The mystery regarding the origin of zoneshifts is even more inscrutable, banished to the oubliettes of imprecision. Are these atypical forces of nature (or culture?) mere offshoots (or strata? or "umbra"?) of timecrashes? Or are they their own organisms, so to speak, generated from an entirely dissimilar trauma? Remember: trauma is the whaleskin of daylight, i.e., trauma is a producing-mechanism without which birth would be a simple matter of receptor nodes and dorsal fins. Nobody knows. A zoneshift has never occurred in the absence of a timecrash, even though the latter has occurred in the absence of the former with dire regularity. And yet a hypothetical answer to the second question can (not) be proven or disproven in the same fashion as a hypothetical answer to the first question. Hence the persistence of the second question notwithstanding its sheer absurdity. In other words, to say "everyone is psychotic" is the same thing as saying "everyone is not psychotic." Hence the problem of carbide subjectivity...

CURTAIN

Act 2

He awakens in slow motion, running across an unformulated vastness...He tries to run faster but it's no use. The faster he runs, the harder gravity pulls...Vague glimpses of a thermogenic corridor. Strobes. Formless shadows yawn into the silhouettes of monsters. Debris on the checkered floor. At the end of the corridor, a vortex glows and grows larger and larger and suddenly he accelerates and slips from slowtime into realtime into fastime and plunges into the vortex...

He finds himself in a white room...in a white hospital gown... strapped onto a padded white mattress raised to a steep incline. Cabinets. Sink. One window, near the ceiling — a rectangle of Blue latticed by thin tracts of barbwire.

He hears voices outside. German. And some other language. Slavic... He tests his binds. They are secure, fixed by metal clamps and reinforced in places with nylon skirt ties and padlocks.

He can escape. He calculates that it would take him no more than ten seconds. Maybe eight. Just as he has developed a proficiency in the martial arts - despite adverse macrobiotic transformations, despite the cirrhotic fabric of the spacetime continuum — so has he developed a taste for escapology, studying the subject voraciously in his spare time, and even composing a doktoral dissertation on Harry Houdini vis-à-vis the theoretical application of various Jeet Kune Do techniques in conjunction with the magician's death by peritonitis, which was caused by a student punching him too many times,

with too much force, in the stomach. The as-of-yet unfinished
dissertation is the product of work at three universities,
one of which he destroyed by turning into Kyoto, the others
shirked by TIMECRASHES. Circumstances providing, he plans
to enroll at Dartmouth as a Ph.D. candidate in either the
Philosophy or English department, preferably in the twenty-
first or twenty-second century, but he will settle for whatever
he can get, and if he manages to obtain candidacy in the late
nineteenth or, better yet, the early twentieth century, he
might have the opportunity to interview Houdini, and possibly
even punch him, on the condition that he can somehow find his
way to Hungary, or track him down on a world tour.

Of course, such activity resists commonsensical meatspace.
In the real world, LOMAN would not concern himself with
trifles. He would focus on day-to-day rituals and essentials
— on getting food, on getting clothes and shelter, on
staying alive. Nor, in the real world, would a stageplay
unfold in this fashion, discussing the psychodiegetics of a
character with such Swiftian, if not Rousseauian, abandon,
while calling attention to itself as a stageplay to boot...

BLANKETY BLANK ensues when eternity eclipses reality.
Anything is possible in the train of metaphysical
annihilation. Acclimatize.

(Image of a maglev gaining momentum as it careens around
the event horizon of a black hole. Plumes of grey residua
churn from chic, streamlined blowholes.)

...LOMAN elects not to escape. The scenario will play out.
Somebody has taken certain efforts to confine him. Or not.

The TIMECRASH *may have detained him. No way to gauge what happens between the sheets.*

The door opens behind LOMAN *and three men enter the room.*

The first man wears a tight-fitting lab coat with sharp, protracted shoulders. The nub of his canary yellow tie forms a perfect triangle. His jetblack hair looks plastic with a kendoll gleam and flawless part on the left side of the skull. Crooked front teeth render a stupid yet insidious grin. He is seven and a half feet tall. This is DR. JOSEF MENGELE.

The second man is short, bald, spectacled, henpecked, zombified. Crease in the chin. Stethoscope around the neck. This is MIKLOS NYISZLI, *assistant to* DR. MENGELE.

The third man is shrunken, emaciated, starved to the bone – an insect on hind legs. Chains rattle from his wrists and ankles. Three vertebrae have ruptured the paperthin skin of his back. This is a POLISH JEW.

DR. MENGELE *chainsmokes cigarettes from an intricate black Bakelite holder that accommodates three cigarettes at a time and never leaves his mouth. Whenever an ember ceases to pulse,* MIKLOS NYISZLI *lights a fresh cigarette and replaces the smoldering butt with remarkable sangfroid.*

DR. MENGELE *sounds like a chicken, reedy and erect, as if always on the verge of clucking. He speaks in German but* LOMAN *understands him; the last time he awakened in the twenty-fifth century, a "lynch mob" of ta moko fetishists implanted a babelfish in his frontal lobe that authorized*

him to translate most major languages into English. Lips
moved and spoke the Other. But he heard the Self.

DR. MENGELE [*bug-eyed*] Yes. Here we are. Welcome back to
    consciousness.

LOMAN   [*apathetically*] Where am I?

DR. MENGELE [*cocking his head*] You speak the English. I
    see. I speak the English as well. But I will
    continue to speak the German. *The German.*

LOMAN   Where am I? Who are you?

DR. MENGELE [*puffing, puffing, puffing*] Auschwitz. My name is
    Doktor Josef Mengele. They call me the "Angel of
    Dracula." These are Jews.

[*The Nazi studies his companions.* MIKLOS NYISZLI *rearranges
his lips. The* POLISH JEW *bows his head.* LOMAN *makes a frog
face.*]

LOMAN   [*to* DR. MENGELE] I've heard of you. I did a research
    paper on you once at the Gymnasium...Josef Mengele
    didn't speak English. He wasn't as tall as you
    either. You're Nephilim. Mengele was a little
    man — five and a half feet high at best. And
    your nickname isn't the "Angel of Dracula." It's
    the "Angel of Death." You must be a temporal
    aberration. A different version of yourself. Like
    everybody.

DR. MENGELE [*puffing, puffing, puffing*] Research paper? Yes, well...We found you outside. You were shitting in the dirt. Like a dog. You were wearing a bustle and makeup. Like a bitch. You were delirious and inarticulate. We suspected you might be a circus clown. We sedated you and we bathed you. Thusly [*gestures in a way that signifies the process of bathing somebody*]. So, again, here we are. I wonder where you came from. I wonder who brought you here. Or what.

LOMAN   The timecrash brought me here. The zoneshift brought me here. They bring everybody everywhere. And nowhere.

DR. MENGELE [*surprised*] Ah! You understand the German. That is good. Yes, yes. Whatever you say, then. Enough smalltalk. Smalltalk is for browbeaten cunts and half-baked porkswords, as they say. How you got here is not important. You are here, yes? That is what matters. Now then. Here is what is going to happen. I will—

LOMAN   [*deadpan*] I am going to kill you.

[*Following a serrated pause,* DR. MENGELE *responds to the interruption with a sharp, awkward blast of laughter. Then he peers querulously at* LOMAN. *Veiled terror marks his gaze. The* POLISH JEW *grins like a skull.* MIKLOS NYISZLI *clears his throat and prepares fresh cigarettes.*]

DR. MENGELE [*nervously, with deferred confidence*] Yes. Well. That is a definitively interesting assertion. One might expect such an assertion from one in your

position. The catastrophe of desperation compels
you...This is what I see. This is the future. I will
execute this Jew, here, now, in front of your eyes, in
order to gauge your reaction. Among my many scientific
exploits, I am admittedly obsessed with how the human
subject reacts to perceived violence. I believe you
are a twin, latent or otherwise — the creases in
your palms and the camber of your perineum suggest a
glib dizygotism. I cannot discern whether or not you
are a Jew. We have taken physiognomic measurements
of your nose and skull and they are of a medium
build, and your brown eyes belie your blonde locks,
which may or may not have been dyed blond. Like the
manner in which you arrived at Auschwitz, however,
your race is of no consequence. I sincerely do not
care who is the Jew and who is not the Jew. My only
concern is for the human body, despite the fact that
we Germans do not recognize the Jew body as a human
body, but secretly I do not subscribe to this manner
of disavowal. An Aryan would suit me just as well as
a Jew, or a Spaniard, or a Martian. *Es geht auf diese
Weise*. [Untranslatable static.] We have attached a
"Hellraiser" electrode to a carefully selected soft
spot on your cranium that will record brain activity.
I applied said moniker to that electrode myself.
Dreams of cenobites harrow me to no end. The brain
activity that we expect to materialize will no doubt
differ from that which would materialize if I had not
told you that I was going to kill this Jew. Nor, for
that matter, would it materialize in the same fashion
had I not told you about my oneiric relationship
with cenobites. Cause and effekt. Cause, I say –

and effekt. And yet it is my contention that the technical application of the element of surprise is pusillanimous, manipulative, rude, and contrary to the principles of *wütende Wissenschaft*. And now I shall slaughter this Jew, lest my superiors unleash a death-monkey with my name on it.

[*It takes* LOMAN *six seconds to escape the apparatus.* DR. MENGELE *observes him in grim amazement. But it is too late for the* POLISH JEW. DR. MENGELE *clicks his fingers and* MIKLOS NYISZLI, *at the ready, drives an irrigation syringe into his chest cavity and hammers down the plunger. The* POLISH JEW'*s skin turns metallic grey and he vomits like an exorcised Catholic. He collapses. Deflates. The open wounds on his spine leak a quiet green fluid...Despite* DR. MENGELE'*s monstrous height,* LOMAN *makes quick work of him. In one kicking motion, he breaks the Nazi's knees, then swings up and roundhouses* MIKLOS NYISZLI *across the chin, cracking his neck with a vulgar report. The assistant throws his arms overhead and topples to the floor, dead.* DR. MENGELE *shrieks at half capacity, somehow continuing to grip the cigarette holder with his lips and inhale smoke...*LOMAN *slaps the cigarettes from his mouth.* DR. MENGELE *shrieks at full capacity now, hot and wet, lips colorless, epiglottis rattling against the hard palate like a speedbag...As promised,* LOMAN, *after a prolonged and unnecessary spell, kills the Nazi and turns, once again, to...*]

INFODUMP, OR, THY PILES

Dr. Mengele is not his first victim. In recent eras, he had become a kind of serial killer, consciously and unconsciously. Of course, he had killed thousands of souls every time he transformed into Kyoto, save one occasion when the transformation occurred in the Florida wetlands, demolishing thousands of alligators and swampthings; otherwise it had occurred within urban or suburban space.

He had never turned into Kyoto willfully. It was a psychosomatic affliction that he couldn't control. In human form, however, he had murdered with premeditation and reckoning. He had never murdered people that didn't deserve it and that were not, to his knowledge, cold-blooded murderers themselves, based on acts he had either witnessed himself or seen on History Channel documentaries.

Each transformation had taken its toll on his psyche and emotional spectrum and moral aptitude. So did the timecrashes, molecularizing and molarizing his BwM (Body without Meaning). He had been drowned by over 100 timecrashes in the last year alone.

...pathologized from multiple directions, by multiple forces...sufficiently unhinged and psychotic. But functional. Functionality was in fact epidemic. He knew he wasn't special with respect to timecrashes. Everybody who endured them became a creature of schizophrenia. The narrative of life inscribed and spoke the living, not vice versa - i.e., a (Low)Man didn't live life, life lived the (Low)Man. Every moment guaranteed the loss of some particle of individual and collective

identity. And yet loss can foster the machinery
of identity-construction. To lose something is
to describe oneself. To lose everything is to
become a complete being. This is the creed of
the numeric system, the code that binds/defines
us. Without ZERO, the system would fail...

Requiem

*...until he arrived at the city limits of Berlin and was
shot in the leg by a gatekeeper. His eyes glowed red, there
was a piercing whistle, and the architecture of his flesh
flowed across the city, obliterating it like a solar flare...
Later, the newspapers attributed the holocaust in Berlin
to the Russians...*

It was the tenth time he turned into Kyoto, and

CURTAIN

七

the 15th time I turned into kyoto
NEWSPAPER AD

TROUBLE METAMORPHOSING INTO KYOTO?

Does metamorphosing into Kyoto fan the flames of arthritis? Do you wish the metamorphosis wasn't so unpredictable, impulsive, and boorish? Would you prefer to be able to control the metamorphosis so that you may, at the very least, become the headstrong author of your own inevitable pain? At this point you cannot control it. When your body tells your brain it is in danger, you become the city. Granted, what constitutes being in danger has metamorphosed for you. You used to fly into a rage when strangers' gazes fluctuated and they looked askance at you, for instance, and on occasion you confronted, even threatened and belittled those strangers, who regarded you in *de facto* disbelief, wondering what they had done wrong. Now you scarcely recognize the existence of strangers, whether their gaze metamorphoses vis-à-vis your BwM or not. And so the corporeal metamorphosis (viz., *metromorphia*) has begotten a psychological and emotional metamorphosis. And so, in simplest terms, change begets change. But that doesn't mean you have to be Change's lapdog. For an unprecedented one-time price of only $29.99 in 5000 easy monthly installments, we offer you agency from the manacles of unbridled selfhood.

Just look at this satisfied customer:

Any dimestore mannequin can see that this young rascal is the very definition of Happiness and Innocence. You too can be happy and innocent again, despite massive stimulation of hangnails and nociceptors. Metamorphosing into Kyoto doesn't have to be such an unpleasant experience. And it doesn't have to be out of your control. Fascist Flesh can help. It's fun to wear Fascist Flesh! Apply the unit as if it might be a cashmere bathrobe you slip into after a hot shower on a winter morning. Allow the unit to adapt to your skin, invade your pores, and gauge the temperament of your blood, bone marrow, and DNA. A slight itching sensation may be followed by suicidal agony. But within seconds—minutes or hours, on occasion—Fascist Flesh will become one with you, and your metamorphosis will be significantly metamorphosed with respect to the way in which you experience and, gentle consumer, wield it, no matter how many times you have turned into Kyoto, whether it be 100 times, or 100,000 times, or two times, or fifteen times...

It was the fifteenth time he turned into Kyoto.

八

the 26th-170th time I turned into Kyoto

DIAGNOSTIC PROSE

...the twenty-fifth time he had turned into Kyoto, and back again. Cognitive estrangement dissolves into straightlaced scaremongering. He blinks...in the late twenty-first century, where Nazisploitation splatterschtick cinema has not only become a cultural norm but the dominant form of cultural capital. Everybody unemployed by Hitler's posthumous and haunted "Single Digit" Corporation suffers constant ridicule and develops supernatural insecurities.

Credits soar onto the page dragging long blue trailers in their wake, as in *Superman* (1978), only the credits also bleed from hideous gunshot wounds...Suddenly the producers realize that this aberration is neither a screenplay nor a film. Embarrassed, they retreat to a gentlemen's club to discuss future creative content over Old Fashions and Manhattans. Onstage, state-of-the-art strippers do listless Time Warps, weighted to the earth by Barsoomian implants...

—The first thing we need to do is put a fuck scene in there, says **Ira Überstein**, fingering a wayward toupee. What's the main guy's name again? Buck? What is this, a science fiction picture? Science fiction is for fags. We need to change that name pronto. Well, let's do the fuck scene first. Here's what I suggest...

Elsewhere, Buck unexpectedly bifurcates into 144 different versions of himself...

Back up. Backup. Bckp.

...He acquires the prostitute from an ALDI with money he makes panhandling banned scikungfi moves to naïve yuppie teenagers looking for a quick high. It's a Septimus-6 model, somewhat *de rigueur*, yet ruinously outdated, an incongruity among anomalies, and therefore "ordinary," square as a misplaced idiom, if not utterly *taedio afficitur*...As the "Austrian Oak" contends:

—The worst thing I can be is the same as everybody else.

—Yeah, that's true, drones **Überstein**. Then allude to Huxley or some shit.

Alphas and Betas and a Brave New Bogarts…What about a gynoid? No narrative is a narrative without a sequined gynoid to stare at. Looks like Viriginia Woolf, this one. Ha. Yeah. Only without the big nose and give her some big tits and a good fucking body. Jesus. And shave that preternatural bush into a nice trim landing strip. If it's a merkin, torch it like a marmot that bit off your finger. Mind the overlip, too, and somebody teach her how to work a stripper pole…

Plate 2.XX: A topless Mrs. Dalloway with flower stems clenched between nicotine-stained dentures swings around the Golden Rod like a teenage gymnast. Illustration courtesy of the Genetic Edition of "Bada Bing Woolf" (Longface Collection).

…He watches idly as an enormous hydraulic smart-arm removes the Maria from a sepulcher on an upper shelf. Another, more delicate smart-arm secures Buck and the lovebirds are ferried to a private red room with velvet walls and a heart-shaped bed sheathed in plastic. Buck flips a switch on the back of the Maria's neck and tells it to lie down on the bed and spread its legs. The legs creak open like a door in the House of Usher. Buck takes off his clothes and sizes up the machinic terrain…No foreplay. He climbs atop the robot and accesses the Primary Text. He makes love to it, spinning it onto all fours and infiltrating the Secondary Text. The robot is voluptuous, with large sagging breasts and a beautiful round ass; he can readily grab the synthetic flesh of its hips as he thrusts his member into it from behind, asking if the robot likes his member, and if it wants more of his member, and if it has ever experienced a member quite like this Kantian thing-in-itself, this noumenon.

—The noumenon, drones the robot in an electric whirr. The noumenon. The noumenon.

—Don't you think a willful use of the slang term *noumenon* in reference to the penis, particularly an erect penis, is stupid? asks Buck in a colloquial tone, thrusting harder, reducing the Secondary Text to a splotch of barcodes and chickenscratches. Then again, the act of sex is stupid in itself. So is the importance many subjects place on sex. Freuds come to strict attention, bury themselves in grassy knolls, and subjects make funny faces—that's sex.

He slaps the Maria's dire flipside.

—Sometimes this stupidity produces offspring between fertile humans. Usually it is enacted for recreational purposes. My point is simple. Noumena belong to philosophy. They don't fuck things.

The Maria nearly bites its lip off when it cums. Vascularized fat—pungent to the taste—fills its mouth and flows onto the bed in thick strands.

Buck yanks himself free, flips the Maria onto its back, and reengages in a detailed analysis of the Primary Text.

The prostitute's eyelids flutter closed. It smiles and savors the afterglow of orgasm, wrapping its legs around Buck and pulling him closer, deeper, ensuring that he writes his opus with precision and flair and ample metaviolence…

Ira Überstein sips a crystal snout of Turkish coffee. Too fucking hot. He burns the roof of his mouth.

—Fuuuck!

A breathless assistant hurries into the office. **Überstein** kidney-punches him and tells him to eighty-six the Turkish coffee and bring him an iced mocha. He withdraws the order, bashes the assistant's head in with a computer keyboard, and exiles him from the gentlemen's club.

Überstein turns to the board of directors with a primal growl.

—All right what the fuck are we gonna do about this fuck scene? Where do we go from here, I mean?

The response is an epidemic of wrinkled, pensive frog faces on popsicle sticks.

Überstein grinds knuckles into eye sockets. He groans and says:

—Thank you for that cornucopia of ideas. As always, your intellects glint like tupperware. You dildos make seven figures a year and you can't even figure out what to do with two pairs of genitals. Christ. I'd be surprised if you milquetoasts knew how to hold your dicks and make a urinal shine. I gotta do everything myself. So be it. So this fuck scene is gonna be real graphic, like. Borderline XXX with lots of tits and ass and bush shots, but no showing the piledriver, only the balls, and only for a flash, like, for half a second, and make sure those goddamned balls are shaved; we can't rightly shove a pair of hairy balls in everybody's faces. Right. So he's fucking this mechabitch, okay? Halfway through let's have the protagonist fracture into 144 different versions of himself, all of whom continue to buttfuck the robot or whatever. Not sure how this is going to work. Not sure why he breaks into 144 versions of himself either. There's some kind of Biblical significance connected to 144, I think. Yeah? Attribute it to a timecrash/zoneshift. Always attribute things we don't feel like explaining to timecrash/zoneshifts. Let's call those TCZs from now on—that's what they call them in the news, and it never hurts to exercise mediatized verisimilitude, even though sex is almost invariably a matter of sheer fantasy. Right. So there's this schizo gangbang thing going on or whatever. In the end, the different versions of Buck accomplish orgasm in unison, short-circuiting the Maria. Also in unison...

...they become 144 versions of Kyoto. They all stand, extremities flaccid, and their eyes roll back into their heads, and their eyes glow white, whiter, whiter still, and the smoldering luminescence blurs the contours of their BwMs, dissolving the meaningless flesh, and the stick figures beneath the surface pulse and contort and discharge technologized screeches that skyrocket and shatter glass and brick and plasteel with equal *joie de vivre*... Barbaric yawps. The rooftops, sharp and gold, pulverize the Maria, and its light goes out in a quiet spray of ersatz nuts and bolts...The rooftops butt heads like *ganado bravo* in a tauromachic battle royal, snorting, growling, bucking for (de)territorialization...ARCHITECTUALYPSE...Like a rash in fasttime, the Kyotos spread across the entire state and leak into several adjacent states, bulldozing animate and inanimate objects...

Dust rises. The sky turns deep red. It always turns some shade of red.

Tranquility.

In the past, on a different continent, Dr. Josef Mengele overdoses on Elective Madness, carefully saws off a boy's skull, and draws pictures with his fingertips in the thin film of mucous that covers the brain tissue. The boy tells him he can feel it. Dr. Mengele concludes that his brain is an impractical repository of livewire nerve endings.

...voice of **Ira Überstein** squelches in the Distance:

—We can do better than that! That's shitty fucking writing. How about some goddamn melody, for fuck's sake? And what's this shit with Mengele? That doesn't have anything to do with anything. There has to be a story, at least, with a beginning and a middle and an end. Like the real world. Like life. People are born and they live and they fuck and act like assholes and then they die. Narrative needs to function that way, too. You can't go in different directions and you can't go backwards or sideways or whatever. And you can't just stick a Nazi up the plot's ass. Figure it out, dipshits. Otherwise this picture's gonna tank. Otherwise...

It was the twenty-sixth through the 170th time he turned into Kyoto.

九

the 202nd time i turned into kyoto

SITCOM SCRIPT

EPISODE 12: THE CITY HUNTER

FADE IN:

SCENE D

INT.CYRANO NIGHTRANGER'S APARTMENT.KITCHEN - DAY

A CUBE OF BUTTER SLOWLY MELTS AND SPREADS TO THE EDGES
OF A PAN. CRACKING SOUND. A RAW EGG FALLS INTO THE PAN
AND BEGINS TO FRY. HOLD THIS SHOT FOR 20-25 MINUTES
UNTIL THE EGG HAS BLACKENED BEYOND RECOGNITION.

[LAFF TRACK]

CYRANO NIGHTRANGER (40s) SURVEYS THE DAMAGE. HE
IS ATTRACTIVE AND SHARP-FEATURED WITH WEATHERED,
SANDBLOWN SKIN. HE WEARS TIGHT-FITTING BLACK JEANS
AND ROCKMOUNT SHIRT AND A PLASTIC LOBSTER APRON.
CONSTERNATION IN HIS EYES. IT IS AS IF HE DOESN'T
KNOW WHY THE EGG BURNED.

    [LAFF TRACK. ONE MAN IN THE AUDIENCE GUFFAWS
    OVER THE LAFFTER OF EVERYBODY ELSE.]

ENTER DICK DALLAS (40s), THE NEIGHBOR. UNLIKE CYRANO,
WHO SMACKS OF THE FUTURISTIC, DICK IS A THROWBACK TO

THE 70S — HAIR LIKE A CROUCHING BEAVER, BUSHY OFF-KILTER MUSTACHE, GIANT COLLAR, WHITE BELLBOTTOMS, SHINY INDIGO PLATFORM SHOES.

                    DICK
          Hey Jack.

                    CYRANO
                    (IRKED)
          My name isn't Jack. It's Cyrano.
          You know my name.

                    DICK
          I know I know it. I call everybody
          Jack, Jack. You know I do that.

FROM THIS POINT ONWARDS, CYRANO NIGHTRANGER WILL BE KNOWN AS JACK NIGHTRANGER.

                    JACK
                    (VACUOUSLY)
          Yeah. I know you do that.

                    DICK
               (SIPPING A HARVEY WALLBANGER)
          What are you doing?

                    JACK
          I'm deciding what to do with this
          egg. I cooked it.

HE TAKES THE PAN BY ITS HANDLE AND SHOWS IT TO DICK.

IMPRESSED, DICK NODS. <u>JACK EXERCISES HIS LIPS</u> AND RETURNS THE PAN TO THE STOVE.

FIVE MINUTES OF DITHYRAMBIC SILENCE PASS. THE NEIGHBORS STARE AND SMILE AT EACH OTHER FIRST, BUT THAT GETS AWKWARD, AND THEIR GAZES BEGIN TO DART AROUND THE ROOM, FINALLY COMING TO REST ON THEIR TOES. VIEWERS WONDER IF THE ACTORS HAVE FORGOTTEN THEIR LINES.

            INFODUMP, OR, THY PILES
      THE SITCOM IS LIVE. DIRECTORIAL
      INTERFERENCE IS PROHIBITED. THE
      SUBTITLE OF THE SITCOM IS: "LIVE,
      RAW, UNCUT, REAL, NO SHIT."

                  DICK
               (BORED)
      Wanna get some hookers?

            INFODUMP, OR, THY PILES
      THIS IS HOW IT ALWAYS STARTS...AND
      ENDS. PRODUCERS HAVE WRITTEN IT INTO
      THE CONTRACT. THE SHOW MUST CULMINATE
      IN PROSTITUTION.

                  JACK
      Maybe. I should figure out this
      egg thing first, though.

[LAFF TRACK. THE SAME MAN GUFFAWS OVER THE LAFFTER OF EVERYBODY ELSE AGAIN. WHEN THE

LAFFTER STOPS, SOMEBODY IN THE AUDIENCE MAKES
A SNIDE REMARK ABOUT HIM.]

DICK DOESN'T KNOW WHAT ELSE TO SAY. HE FINISHES THE
HARVEY WALLBANGER, MAKES A TEQUILA SUNRISE ON A SMALL
VERANDA BAR, AND TURNS ON A WALLSCREEN. HE ASKS THE
WALLSCREEN TO SHOW HIM THE PORNO CHANNELS. HE GETS
BORED AND TELLS IT TO GO TO A NEWS CHANNEL.

NEWSCASTER <u>BING DINGALING</u> (50s) HEATEDLY REPORTS ON THE
RECENT EXPLOITS OF A DERANGED ENGLISH PROFESSOR, DR.
BLAH BLAH BLAH, AND HIS PSYCHOTIC 'GÄNGER, DR. IDENTITY,
TOGETHER KNOWN AS "THE DYSTOPIAN DUO," AMONG OTHER
SOBRIQUETS, WHO, FOR REASONS "DISTURBINGLY UNKNOWN,"
HAVE COMMENCED A BLOODY KILLING SPREE OF "OUTRAGEOUS
PROPORTIONS." A TOOTHPASTE COMMERCIAL GRIN PUNCTUATES
THE DEEP BRONZE SKIN OF BING'S FACE. HIS DOMINANT FEATURES
INCLUDE TWO WINGTIP WIZARD-OF-OZ EYEBROWS AND THREE
SURGICALLY IMPLANTED DIMPLES ONTO CHEEKS AND CHIN.

                        BING
                     (HAPPILY)
          According to this shocking news-
          flash I'm receiving via occipital
          lobe, moments ago Dr. Identity was
          digitized in the heinous act of
          mass murder. Among the dead are
          Papanazis, an abominable snowman,
          six Frankenstein monsters, three
          grandmothers, countless Pigs, and a
          Tyrannosaurus Rex that the 'gänger
          executed by ripping its jaws into

two pieces and forthwith yanking
out the great lizard's bowels by
the tongue. Authorities agree that
something must be done about this
vile incursion of unprecedented
bleep, but nobody knows where to
begin. The android and its prototype seem altogether impervious to
FDA approved brands of social etiquette. Alternate means of negotiating this holocaustic behavior
must be devised immediately. More
on this disturbing and outlandish
story as it continues to unfold.

DICK WATCHES THE NEWSCAST WITH ESCALATING CURIOSITY.
JACK HAS REMOVED A CARTON OF EGGS FROM THE REFRIGERATOR.
HE INSPECTS THE TEXTURE OF THE SHELLS.

DICK AND JACK AND BING SUDDENLY RAISE THEIR ARMS AND
FREEZE IN MIMELIKE POSES OF TERROR, AS IF MARTIANS ARE
ATTACKING AND THEY ARE CHARACTERS IN AN ED WOOD FILM.
THEY STRIKE THE POSES FOR 5 MINUTES. RED STATIC SLOWLY
ENGULFS THE SCREEN, BLEEDING FROM THE CORNERS, UNTIL
WE CAN'T SEE ANYTHING, AND THE SOUND OF THE STATIC
RISES TO A BLARING CRESCENDO. HOLD FOR 15 MINUTES. THE
STATIC RETREATS TO THE SCREEN CORNERS AND WE RETURN
TO JACK NIGHTRANGER'S KITCHEN. DICK AND JACK SPEAK TO
EACH OTHER IN FASTTIME, VOICES LIKE EXCITED MICE. BING
DOESN'T SAY ANTHING: HE STARES BLANKLY INTO THE CAMERA
WAITING FOR THE TÊTE-À-TÊTE TO END.

IT ENDS. <u>FASTIME SLAMS INTO REALTIME</u>.

> BING
> (GLUMLY)
> In other holocaust-related news, the Kyoto Man has struck again. Current estimates gauge his aggression at over 200 genocides. The Dystopian Duo doesn't hold a candle to this **bleep**'s slit-eyed cruelty. Tens of thousands have perished in his wake, often in one fell swoop. The spatialities of Quebec City and Belfast no longer exist except as vast meteor craters. Rumor has it that the Kyoto Man also destroyed Bath in the seventeenth century, but written accounts of the scandalous devastation differ, some witnesses attributing the loss of the city to a *daikaiju*, others to various natural disasters.

AS BING REPORTS THE STORY, JACK BECOMES AGITATED. HE ABANDONS THE EGGS AND TURNS HIS ATTENTION TO THE WALLSCREEN.

> DICK
> (CONCERNED)
> What's wrong, Jack?

[LAFF TRACK]

                    JACK

I know him. The Kyoto Man. That's
the man I'm tracking. That's the
city they paid me to kill.

                 [LAFF TRACK]

                    DICK
                  (PENSIVE)
I wonder if the real Kyoto still
exists.

                 [LAFF TRACK]

                    JACK

Nobody knows. The region in Japan
where the real Kyoto used to
be turned into a black hole or
something. It's like a big **bleeping**
cloud or something. Nobody can see
anything. Not even with cameras.
Search parties go in and never
come out. It eats people. Like
the Bermuda Triangle.

                 [LAFF TRACK]

                    DICK

That's   a   myth.   The   Bermuda
thing.

                 [LAFF TRACK]

                    JACK
Triangle.

              [LAFF TRACK]

                    DICK
  (CONCILIATORY, THEN NONPLUSSED)
Yeah, that's right... What? What
are we talking about?

              [LAFF TRACK]

                    JACK
Kyoto. How it's a **bleeping bleep**.

              [LAFF TRACK]

                    DICK
Oh yeah...I knew that. I...

              [LAFF TRACK]

                    JACK
  (OUTRAGED AT THE LAFF TRACK)
Shut the **bleep** up! I'm listening
to this **bleeping bleep**!

[LAFF TRACK. THE SAME MAN GUFFAWS OVER THE LAFFTER
OF EVERYBODY ELSE YET AGAIN — HE HAS BEEN GUFFAWING
THROUGHOUT THE CONVERSATION. SOMEBODY PUNCHES
HIM. WE HEAR THE SHARP CRACK OF BONE AGAINST BONE.
THE MAN CRIES OUT AND FALLS SILENT.]

[LAFF TRACK]

BING

...whirlwind thinktanks claim he can now control his affliction, unlike the buzz of antiquity, which called him a victim of metromorphia. Therefore the frothing genocide he commits is not calculated, but deliberate. *The Guiness Book of World Recalcitrants* has deemed him History's Greatest Terrorist. **Bleep** me. Moreover, the preliminary extracts of Herman Melville's *Moby-Dick* have been amended to include the following passage, allegedly in reference to the Awful Beast:

"In the time beyond time, Leviathan stalked across the universe, exorcising his blowhole against the fury of human scrimmage."

The Law has placed a bounty on the head of this extravagant wretch and encourages vigilantism of any kind until the monstrous vermin is put down like the rabid dog he is.

DICK

How much are they paying you?

JACK

A lot. A lot up front and a lot at
the back door. I'm not the only one.
Uncle Samsara is cutting checks
to any **bleep** who promises to hunt
down the Kyoto Man. 8.000 creds per
bleep, I think. For professional
bounty hunters it's much more. I
got to find this **bleeping** weirdo.

DICK
(FINISHING THE TEQUILA SUNRISE)
How're you gonna do that?

[LAFF TRACK]

[LAFF TRACK]

[BEAT]

[LAFF TRACK]

A TIMECRASH COINCIDES WITH A ZONESHIFT AND METASTASIZES
INTO A PSYCHOSHOP. FOR TEN SECONDS, EVERYBODY IN THE
SHOW AND EVERYBODY WATCHING THE SHOW EXISTS INSIDE
THE HEAD OF CAPTAIN AHAB (LATE 50s).

AHAB
(RUBBING THE KNEE ABOVE HIS PEG LEG)
Goddamn this arthritis. Pass me
that analgesic, Starbuck. The
tube of Bengué. Aye.

GLOBAL DISEMBODIMENT OF CONSCIOUSNESS...

                    BING
          (WITH GUARDED EXHILIRATION)
        And now this schizercial break.

RUN SIXTEEN SCHIZERCIALS. ONE OF THEM SHOULD FEATURE
A BEAUTIFUL ANTHROPOMORPHOUS AND TENTACLED PRINCESS
À LA EDGAR RICE BURROUGHS. JACK REGARDS THE PRINCESS
LIKE A FRESH CADAVER.

                    DICK
              (MAKING A B-52)
        So what did we decide about those
        hookers?

                [LAFF TRACK]

                    JACK
        Forget about that, Dick. Look at
        this **bleep**. Listen to this **bleep**.

                    BING
                 (DEADPAN)
        ...an interview with a middle-aged
        peregrinator who claims to be the
        Kyoto Man. Dominique Erstwhile is
        with that peregrinator, now, live,
        in Picadilly Circus. Dominique?

MIDNIGHT IN LONDON. THICK DRIZZLE. BLADERUNNERLIKE
PANORAMA OF BROBDIGNAGIAN ELECTRONIC MEDIA. WAR

CORRESPONDENT <u>DOMINIQUE ERSTWHILE</u> (30s) WEARS AN
AVENGERS-STYLE BOWLER HAT AND SUIT AND HOLDS A SPIKED
UMBRELLA. NEXT TO HIM STANDS "THE KYOTO MAN" (40s),
WHO MAY OR MAY NOT BE "<u>THE KYOTO MAN</u>." HE IS AN
ORDINARY-LOOKING WHITE MALE WEARING DARK JEANS AND A
PLAIN GREEN FLAK JACKET.

> DOMINIQUE
> (DIS/POSSESSED)
> Thank you, Bing. I'm here with
> the Kyoto Man.

> [LAFF TRACK]

THE LAFF TRACK ABRUPTLY THREADS FROM LAFFTER INTO
COUGHING AND THEN CHOKING AND GASPING. THE CHARACTERS
IN EPISODE 12, ON AND OFF THE WALLSCREEN, WAIT
PATIENTLY FOR THE LAFF TRACK TO DIE.

IT DIES. THE REMAINDER OF THE EPISODE IS ACCOMPANIED
ONLY BY TWO INSTANCES OF UNCANNY SILENCE JUST A FEW
BEATS FROM THIS POINT IN THE SCRIPT.

> "THE KYOTO MAN"
> (ACIDLY)
> I'm not the Kyoto Man.

> DOMINIQUE
> (STUNNED)
> No? This is not correct information.
> This is not the information,
> sir. If you're not the Kyoto

Man, who are you? What's your
name?

                  "THE KYOTO MAN"
Everybody wants to know everybody's
name. What's the big **bleeping** deal?
I'm a man. That's good enough.

                  DOMINIQUE
A man. A man. Hmm.

              [UNCANNY SILENCE]

                  "THE KYOTO MAN"
Bleep.

                  DOMINIQUE
                  (PENSIVELY)
Let's focus on your hazardous
predicament. You have recently
come out of the closet, so to
speak, and admitted who you are,
even if you refuse to tell us
who you are, other than that you
are, as you say, a "man." That's
fine.

                  "THE KYOTO MAN"
              (RAISING HIS VOICE)
I didn't come out of anything.
I'm a **bleep** on the street.

DOMINIQUE
(BLADE EXTENDING FROM THE UMBRELLA)
Of course you are. And if I cut
you open, blood, not shingles
and straw, will issue from the
cavernous wound. Is that what
we're supposed to believe? Is that
the correct information?

A FEMME DOCILE (20s) APPEARS NEXT TO "THE KYOTO MAN."
SHE IS THIN WITH STRINGY BLONDE HAIR AND WEARS A RAGTAG
TOP AND STRIPED LONGSTOCKINGS. A HEMORRAGE OF MASCARA
IDENTIFIES THE ANGLES OF HER CHEEKBONES. HER BREASTS
ARE TOO FIRM AND CIRCULAR TO BE REAL. WE DON'T KNOW IF
HER SUDDEN PRESENCE IS STAGED OR ACCIDENTAL.

"THE KYOTO MAN" TAKES THE FEMME DOCILE BY THE NECK
AND KISSES HER, SOFTLY AT FIRST, BUT THE KISS BECOMES
MORE FORCEFUL AND VIOLENT, AND THEIR TONGUES ENGAGE
IN A KIND OF WUXIA PIAN DEATH MATCH THAT PRODUCES
SPARKS AND HEAT LIGHTNING.

THE KISS BREAKS WITH A PEEL OF THUNDER AND THE FEMME
DOCILE SLIPS OFFSCREEN.

STONE-FACED, "THE KYOTO MAN" BLUSHES ... THEN GOES
PALE. A BARELY DECIPHERABLE BEAD OF GLOWING PINK
FLUID EMERGES FROM A LIP CORNER, FLOWS DOWN HIS CHIN
AND DRIPS ONTO THE SHOULDER OF HIS FLAK JACKET.

BING LOOKS ASKANCE AT "THE KYOTO MAN."

[UNCANNY SILENCE]

                    JACK
                  (ANXIOUS)
Bleep.   That's   happening   right
now, Dick.

                    DICK
What's happening?

                    JACK
          (PEERING OUT A WINDOW)
Wake up, **bleep**. This interview.
It's happening down the street.

                    DICK
It can't be. It's daytime.

                    JACK
It's nighttime down the street.
Look.

DICK JOINS JACK AT THE WINDOW. PICADILLY CIRCUS IS
JUST A FEW BLOCKS AWAY, SHROUDED IN DARKNESS. AN
ABSTRACT MATHEMATICAL LINE FALLS FROM THE SKY AND
DIVIDES THE DAY FROM THE NIGHT LIKE A PINT OF BLACK
& TAN.

          INFODUMP, OR, THY PILES
"I DO NOT MEAN TO ASK YOU TO ACCEPT
ANYTHING WITHOUT REASONABLE GROUND FOR
IT. YOU WILL SOON ADMIT AS MUCH AS

I NEED FROM YOU. YOU KNOW OF COURSE
THAT A MATHEMATICAL LINE, A LINE OF
THICKNESS *NIL*, HAS NO REAL EXISTENCE.
THEY TAUGHT YOU THAT? NEITHER HAS
A MATHEMATICAL PLANE. THESE THINGS
ARE MERE ABSTRACTIONS." **THE TIME
TRAVELLER**, H.G. WELLS' *THE TIME
MACHINE*

TOGETHER JACK AND DICK TURN AND FACE THE WALLSCREEN.

DOMINIQUE
(CLUTCHING A DEAD THEORY BY THE GILLS)
Are you going to manifest Kyoto
now? Visceral discharge, the keen
viewer realizes, is the prelude
to your loathsome death-kiss. But
I was under the impression that
you could control yourself. You
choose to be a becoming-city. You
choose to wreak architectural
havoc. The element of choice is
under your spell.

"THE KYOTO MAN"
(STRAINING, NECK CORDED)
I know you. And I want nothing to
say to you.

EXT.NEW YORK CITY - DAY/NIGHT

JACK

(HYPERTROPHIC)
That's the wrong city.

EXT.LONDON - DAY/NIGHT

"THE KYOTO MAN" METAMORPHOSES INTO KYOTO, DEMOLISHING
THE GREATER PART OF LONDON. THIS TAKES AWHILE.

EXT.KYOTO - HIGH NOON

SECOND TO LAST SHOT: JACK NIGHTRANGER ESCAPES IN A
MODEST STEAMPUNK BALLOON. A CROWN OF ROPES HANGS FROM
THE CHARIOT, ONE OF WHICH DICK CLINGS TO FOR DEAR LIFE.
HIS WEIGHT THROWS THE VEHICLE OFF BALANCE, SO JACK CUTS
THE ROPE WITH A SURVIVAL KNIFE AND DICK FALLS SCREAMING
INTO A MACHIYA, CRASHING THROUGH THE SHINGLED ROOF,
THEN THROUGH THE PARQUET MAPLE FLOOR OF THE KITCHEN.
FINALLY HE EXPLODES ONTO A JUDO MAT IN THE BASEMENT.

LAST SHOT: SPLATTERSCHTICK IMAGE OF A RAUNCHY-LOOKING
PROSTITUTE SPLAYED OUT ON SILK BEDSHEETS...

BEFORE THE CREDITS ROLL, THIS SCRIPT, ACCOMPANIED BY A
FLOURISH OF BRASS INSTRUMENTS, APPEARS IN RED LETTERING:

IT WAS THE 202ND TIME HE TURNED INTO KYOTO

                                        FADE OUT.

the 250th time I turned into Kyoto

EPISTOLARY PROSE INCL. TITLE PAGE

AN

APOLOGY

FOR THE

LIFE

OF

MR. SOANDSO BLANKETY BLANK.

In which, the many notorious FALSEHOODS and
MISREPRESENTATIONS of a Book called

THE KYOTO MAN,

Are expofed and refuted; and all the matchlefs
ARTS of that middle-aged Metromorph, fet in a true and juft Light.

Together with
A full Account of all that paffed between him
and Various Perfonages; whofe Character is
reprefented in a manner fomething different from
that which he bears in *THE KYOTO MAN.* The
whole being exact Copies of authentick Papers
delivered to the Editor.
Neceffary to be had in all FAMILIES.
By Mr. STANLEY ASHENBACH.

BLIPTOWN:
Printed for S. Pliffken, in New York, without Scruff.
M——MDCCI.

To Miss_____, &c.

Madam:

It will naturally be expected, that when I write the Chapter of my Life entitled "The 250th Time I Turned into Kyoto (Epistolary Prose incl. Title Page)," I should dedicate it to some young Lady, whose Wit and Beauty etc., etc., etc.

...landed on a Comet and experienced sundry Adventures during which Hearts were broken and the Relationship between Nature and Technology was constantly problematized. In retrospect, however, I fear I may have been confusing subjective Reality with the Film *Armageddon*. Did I mention that B. Affleck occupies my Dreams no less than four times a Week? He is invariably gentlemanly and possesses neatly arranged Teeth, albeit I fear he should have the Mole on his right Cheek inspected by a Mole Docktor. What does One call a Mole Docktor? The technical Designation escapes me...

I arrive, then, at the whetted Thrust of my Letter, on the occasion that I, viz., Mr. Soandso Blankety Blank for sake of Argument, traveled to the Year 802,701 A.D. on the Crest of a monstrous TCZ. But are TCZs not all monstrous? It is only a Matter of Degrees and Intensities. Of course, I could not accurately discern if the Year was 802,701 A.D. It might have been 801,702 A.D., or one Year later, or ten thousand Years earlier, and so forth. Nevertheless I had a Feeling it was 802, 701 A.D. And Feelings constitute the Loco-motion of Man. Perception and Reality are only a Matter of that which we *feel* when we are put to the Test. So it goes. Cause and Effekt. *Motus animi continuus.* Everything results from emotive Knee-Jerks. Tests, Existence, Desiring-Production. Everything.

As a matter of course, I scored 956 on my SATs, 18 on my ACTs. I cannot remember what I scored on my GREs. Rest assured it was not worthy of Recollection and the only University that accepted the Sawdust of my Insufficiency was the University I offered to liberate from Bankruptcy. Standardized Testing and I have always been merciless Enemies . . .

Per usual, I emerged into Futurity confused, nauseous, and somewhat depressed, but I told Myself these feelings would pass, and indeed they did, save the Depression, which never passes, but I have grown accustomed to the Blues and reject Medication at every Turn, preferring to suck the Marrow from Life of my own free Will and sound Mind, rather than exist as a doped-up Fleshball from whom the Vampyre of Life sucks whatever it pleases.

(At this Moment, somewhere beyond the Diegesis of this Letter, the cunning Reader detects the Echo of a Pill being swallowed.)

Standing with Arms akimbo on a sloping, sickly Beach, I surveyed the Landscape. A starless Sky hung overhead like endless Whalehide. There was no wind, no sound, no sign of Life. The still, bloodred Water stretched to the Horizon; barely a Ripple disturbed the viscous Skin of its Surface ... I inhaled deeply ... smell of Sulfur, and Salt, and Formaldehyde ... It was at this Juncture, Dear Lady, that I felt the Need to cling to some form of Machinery, anything with Cogs and Sprockets would do, and in that feverish state of Mind, I might have settled for a simple aluminum Flagpole. I imagined what it might be like to embrace my Grandfather's Tractor, that green Behemoth, that *Objectifique* of technologized Masculinity, with its hard black Tyres and smoldering, whistling Pipes, ready to tame Mother Earth, to pry apart her Buttocks and rumble across the Dirt, full Steam ahead—how the cattle used to cringe in fear, emitting feeble moos ...

Initially I assumed that the Landscape was entirely devoid of Life. Even the Pile of Rocks down by the Shoal, I gauged, was sterile and barren—no Moss, no Seaweed, certainly no mindful Creatures, invertebrate or otherwise. It was dark, but not inordinately dark; despite the lack of Stars and Moon, the Sky, while gray in some Places, dark green in Others, released a faint, toxic Glow that cast uncanny Shadows across the Beach. I studied these Shadows for a lengthy Duration, wondering what Things could possibly be responsible for them. Then I heard a dull, pathetic Wail—the kind of Wail that escapes a mutilated Barn Animal on its last Legs.

The Object on the Beach was a round Thing, roughly the size of a Football, perhaps larger. Minced Tentacles extended from its oily Bulk and it hopped to and fro in fits of anger, or anxiety, or the Devil knows what. It looked very much like a Heart that had been yanked out of Somebody's Chest and cast aside, and yet the Heart continued to beat, as if to assure its adversary, "You may wrench me from my host body, yes, you may do that. But I will nonetheless continue with the Business of Diastolic Supremacy. My Ventricles are stronger than your Bullshit." I do not mean to upset the Gentle Miss with graphic metaphors, but I am attempting to be as honest and truthful as a simple Man of the Crowd can be, and figurative Language of the ghastly and disgusting Variety is often the only Means at my Disposal when conveying such Horrors, such Futures, such hopeless Irrealities.

It came to my Attention that there were more than one or two of these peculiar, grimy, and possibly obstreperous Creatures. As I made my way toward the Water's Edge, I perceived in fact that the Beach teemed with them. I grinned. The Grin was altogether unexpected, but I welcomed it, and I plodded forward, unsheathing a Samurai Sword from its leather Housing ... I must have delivered over 600 of them to Eternity. A fluorescent pink Substance erupted from their Hides as I put them, one at a Time, through the Ringer. I wondered momentarily if they were devolved Martians. I also suspected that they might be devolved Artificial Intelligences: several of them revealed their Innards to be Fiberoptics, Nuts and Bolts, Turbochargers, Spools of Tape ... At any Rate, I dispatched them all ...

During the Smoking of a rather enormous yet rather dry Montecrifto, I enjoyed the vifual Spectacle of the Carnage I had induced before falling back into more conventional Modes of urban Alterity, etc. But I had done it all Myfelf, with my own Hand, my own Blade, my own Will to Power...Old Habits are hard to fake, after all...

A moft Obedient, and
obliged humble Servant,
S&S. BLANKETY BLANK

P.S. It was the 250th Time I turned into Kyoto.

＋一

the 257th time i turned into kyoto

CRITERION PROSE

Applying the dominant styles of Michael Jai White, Dr. Gradgrind's favorite actor, they moved through sequences of Shotokan, Goju-ryu, Tang Soo Do, Kyokushin (the actor's most accomplished style), Kobudo (weapons incl. nunchucks, knuckledusters, and canoe oars), Blaxploitarantino Taekwondo, Iaido, and Wushu Kung-Fu.

Dr. Gradgrind struck his opponent in the windpipe with the blade of his hand and brought the fight to an abrupt conclusion.

"Arigato, 'Sid,'" said the doktor, making quote signs with his fingers.

"Sid" choked and passed out. Dr. Gradgrind wondered if he had injured him. Quickfire diagnosis: "Sid" is fucked…

Paramedics were summoned; they enacted hazardous procedures with unsanitized instruments…An orderly caressed his esophagus until he awoke. He pretended to return to consciousness slowly, eyes creasing open, so that he could admire the orderly's cleavage.

"My name isn't 'Sid,'" he whispered. "It's 'Sam.'"

Escorting the orderly to the door, Dr. Gradgrind replied: "'Sam,' 'Sid'—it's all the same. Both signatures begin with the letter 'S.' Both contain three letters—a consonant followed by a vowel followed by another consonant. Both are monosyllabic."

"All true. All invalid."

"As is language. Let's get wet."

Dr. Gradgrind and "Sid" took a shower. They soaped up their extremities with careful gestures, wary of leaving portions of skin unclean. "Sid" couldn't take his eyes off of the doktor's chiseled-from-stone chest. He depressed the nipples to test the equipment's authenticity…Near the end, "Sid" applied eucalyptus-scented exfoliating cream to his palms, elbows, knees and heels…

They sat in their respective chairs.

"I swear," said Dr. Gradgrind, "the older I get, the more hair I grow." He ran a cupped palm from hairline to neckline. "What's the opposite of going bald? Going hairy? Hirsute—that's a more technical term. I'm going hirsute."

"I don't feel well," said "Sid."

"Hard times. That's why you're here."

"I know. I know why I'm here. I mean I don't feel well today. Lately. Ever. I have never felt well."

The doktor flicked lint from his sleeve. "Have you ever been happy? Ever?"

"Sid" snared his lips. Dr. Gradgrind made his hands into a thoughtful teepee.

"Sid" said, "There was a time when I was happy. I remember. I was in the third grade. I went to a wave pool with my friend Andy Conklin. Do you know what a wave pool is?"

"Yes. Yes."

"It's a pool that artificially generates its own waves. The generator is located in the wall of the deep end. It's a kind of accordion device that hurls waves across the surface of the pool to a canal in the shallow end that then reroutes the excess water back to the deep end."

"Yes. Yes."

"The sun felt so good that day. I can remember exactly how it felt if I concentrate hard enough." He concentrated. "I have never experienced anything like the sensation of the cool water against my soft young skin on that summer afternoon. I felt pure and natural and alive and clean. I was happy."

"Happy," ricocheted Dr. Gradgrind. He smiled.

"Sid" smiled. "Comes to mind I was happy on another occasion. It was another summer afternoon and I was eating an ice cream cone. I can't remember what flavor. But there was a gumball at the bottom of the cone. I was happy."

"That's very nice." The doktor collapsed the teepee of his hands and began to exercise his fingers.

"That reminds me of another time I was happy. I guess I've been happy a lot. There was this field of rye. A bunch of kids were playing in it and I was standing on this crazy cliff. If the kids got too near the cliff, I would catch them in a big leather mitt so that they didn't fall over. Every time I caught one, I felt good. I felt happy."

Dr. Gradgrind cleared his throat. "That's from *The Catcher in the Rye*."

"The what?" said "Sid."

"*The Catcher in the Rye*. You know. The business about the children and the cliff. That's a compensatory wish-fulfillment fantasy à la Holden Caulfield, the tormented, adolescent, spiteful protagonist of J.D. Salinger's novel. In the end, you always spiral into some kind of Holden Caulfield-related pity party. That's natural enough. Most of my clients do that."

"You have other clients? I thought I was the only one."

The doktor observed him.

"Sid" observed his lap.

"I think I'm a serial killer," said "Sid."

"Oh," said Dr. Gradgrind. "What makes you think that?"

"I've been killing people. I think."

"You think."

"I've been traveling through time and space, too. I don't know if I'm psychotic or it's the TCZs." "Sid" eyeballed Dr. Gradgrind, taking a deep breath.

"TCZs," remarked Dr. Gradgrind with a pale frown.

He exhaled. "Yeah. It might be real. It might be irreal. It might be nothing."

"Is 'irreal' a word? I believe that's a Portuguese word. Used properly—a Portuguese irregular *verb*."

Long silence. "Sid" reclined on the chaise. Then, in a kind of subterranean voice: "I am a superior person suffering from a nervous breakdown. Or I am an ordinary man suffering from everyday life. Either way, I'm fucked. We're all fucked."

"That's an exciting perspective. Say more. In your normal voice, please. Remember: nothing impresses me, nothing distresses me. Say more now."

"Sid" snorted. "Haven't I said enough?"

The doktor shrugged. "To speak is to fight. Human violence knows no boundaries—it leaps into the atmosphere and charges across the cosmos. Hajime."

"Sid" carried on in a regular tone. "Anyway, in the last chapter...uhm,

last week, I mean, or maybe yesterday, or Thursday, very possibly Thursday...
Vellum. Papyrus...Anyway, I was in the distant future, near the end of the world,
and there were these creatures jumping all over the beach. I assumed they were
devolved humans and dispatched them. I don't know why. I felt like it. And yet the
experience gave me no pleasure. Then I found myself in the past, or the present,
or somewhere, goddamn it, and I dispatched that Nazi doktor, Whatshisname, the
one who keeps showing up in my dreams, which is to say, in my reality."

"Yes. Dreams belong to antiquity. There is only reality. There is only the
cold granite of reality."

"I know, I know. Fuck. So then I dispatched a contingent of Huns who had
ransacked a small village—I felt like Steve McQueen in *Bullitt*—the sky, the
surf, the wind in my hair...Then, somewhere else, a novel I think, or a B-movie
maybe—not the real world, anyhow, but a fictional diegesis that I accidentally
slipped into—I dispatched a fair share of zombies in a mall. I was black. I was
a policeman. In the distance, a fat woman screamed. You know that scream fat
women make? She was alone. Then I remember a Victrola set up in the corner of
a vast waiting room with dull green walls and Old Person chandeliers. Music from
the Jazz Age emanated from the Victrola's fleur-de-lis. I felt like Nick Carraway at
a Gatsby party: inadequate, awkward, destitute, useless, ugly, out-of-shape, dumb.
I used a sledgehammer to dispatch the Victrola, and I also dispatched various
sculptures and paintings, and I treated the Old Person chandeliers like piñatas...I
dispatched hundreds of other people and things, in other spatial and temporal and
narrational contexts. Thousands, really. And that doesn't even account for the
hundreds of thousands of people I have dispatched by way of metamorphosing
into the city of Kyoto. Even you are among my victims. I turned into Kyoto and
dispatched you. Only you had a different name. But I dispatched you."

"And yet here I sit," said Dr. Gradgrind, chewing a fingernail.

"So you say," said "Sid."

"You fight well, young man."

"I'm older than you. Don't call me that."

"You don't like to be called anything. Are you aware of this?"

"I like to be called things that are true. Truth is the thing."

Dr. Gradgrind traced the parameters of his beard with his thumb. "I am at least fifteen years your senior."

Sucking in his cheeks, "Sid" counted something out with his fingers.

"That's enough," said the doktor. "Now then. I'm curious about this excessive use of the term *dispatch*. You employed the term at least fifty times in your last monologue."

"Fifty times? That's crazy. I barely used fifty words."

"*Dispatch*. Why this term? What does it mean to you?"

"I want to talk about...Isn't it strange that I...Isn't it strange that I think I dis...*killed* you? Isn't everything I've told you, like, fucked up? What about Kyoto? Why Kyoto? I don't know shit about Kyoto."

"All you want to talk about is Kyoto." Dr. Gradgrind sighed. "It's redundant. It's not helping the process. The issue has run its course." He leveled his gaze. "*Dispatch*."

"Sid" contemplated fleeing the session. He swung his legs to the floor and placed hands on knees as if to thrust himself onto his feet and march out the door. He had done it before...possibly. Sometimes he remembered doing it before...But he couldn't be certain. He wasn't even certain about the identity of Dr. Gradgrind. He was nominally aware of visiting him, on a regular basis, for years. At the same time, something told him that the therapist was a complete stranger. Or worse—an imposter.

"Do I know you?" Immediately "Sid" couldn't remember if he had spoken the question in his head or aloud.

Dr. Gradgrind's lips mouthed the word: "DIS-PATCH."

"I don't know," groaned "Sid." "I guess *dispatch* sounds better than *kill* or *murder*. Less pedestrian. I don't know why. *Dispatch* is more technical or scientific or something. Ok? Fuck."

Dr. Gradgrind snapped his fingers lightly, rhythmically, with drama. "I'm satisfied. Was that so hard?"

"No."

"Yes. Yes. What next? We've settled 'The Dispatch Matter,' as I will refer to it in my notes." He wrote the title down on a thick pad of faded hemp paper and put a check next to it. "Tell me about your sex life."

"Sex life?" "Sid" shook his head in disbelief. "I'm a virgin. You know I'm a virgin. We talk about it all the time—far more than Kyoto. I suspect that's why you indulge me."

"'The Virgin Matter' is why I indulge you?"

"Fuck you."

"Be nice. Respect your sensei. It's ok. You say you're a virgin."

"Born-again."

"You're not religious. You are in fact as nihilistic as a French *reine de drame* nibbling dry baguettes and sipping cold coffee in a chintzy Algerian café. *Seulement*, of course."

"You don't need to be religious to be a born-again virgin."

"By that logic one can be a born-again anything. I can be a born-again Yakety Yak or a born-again Somethingorother—anything I used to be, from the first glimmer of consciousness, before an *action*"—snatching at the air—"robbed me of it. Very well. But you recognize that this born-again sleight-of-hand is the most embarrassing variety of horseshit conceived by civilized humankind. One is born once. Then one dies. Anybody who professes to be a born-again Yahoo does so for a single reason: to reclaim something lost or stolen from the past. So. Let's start by discussing the last time you made love to a woman. Spare no details. I will know if you leave out the details. Life is nothing without minutia. Tell me everything."

"Fuck off."

Minutes later, "Sid" told him everything. He included all of the details, attended to all of the five senses.

"Brrrrzzzzrrrr," replied Dr. Gradgrind. "This is what we need to flesh out. Your deepest desire. Do you know what it is?"

"I just told you what it is," said "Sid." "I repeated it over and over. You keep asking me to repeat it."

"I'm asking you again. One last time."

"You said 'one last time' last time."

"I really mean it this time. Really—this is the last time."

"Sid" flexed his jaw. "Before I tell you again, I want you to know that I know that this isn't the last time you will ask me what my deepest desire is. I want you to know that I know that."

Dr. Gradgrind shut his eyes and bobbed his head.

"My deepest desire, since childhood, has always been for people to look at me and say: 'Nobody can fuck with that cunt.'"

The doktor observed him.

"I'm getting up." "Sid" stood. "I'm going to walk around. My ass hurts." He paced back and forth. Dr. Gradgrind watched him like a wild animal that had wandered into the office.

"I think somebody's chasing me," said "Sid."

"Yes, you mentioned that," said Dr. Gradgrind.

"I'm mentioning it again, fucker...Sorry. I'm sure somebody is chasing me. At least one man. A bounty hunter. But maybe more than him. Sometimes I feel like the entire human race is chasing me. How do I escape the human race? There's nowhere to hide."

"Mars," the doktor muttered.

"What?"

"Delusions of persecution," the doktor muttered.

"What?"

"Nothing," the doktor muttered.

Two minutes passed.

"When metaphor dies," said "Sid," "what's left?"

Dr. Gradgrind grinned a sadist's grin. "The surface."

"The surface of what?"

"Everything. And nothing."

"That's a copout."

"You are a copout."

Two minutes passed.

"What's your deepest desire?" asked Dr. Gradgrind.

"Sid" walked to a point in the office that he considered to be as far away from the therapist as possible. "To exist," he said.

"Precisely. But existence isn't enough. Ergo." He held out his left palm and walked across it with the index and middle fingers of his right hand. He did this carefully, as if the fingers were made of glass and might break.

Two minutes passed.

"What's your deepest desire?" asked Dr. Gradgrind.

"Are you familiar with the concept of scikungfi?" replied "Sid." "It is a purely linguistic formation."

"You are a linguistic formation."

"What does that mean?"

"Is that a rhetorical question?"

"Is that a rhetorical question?"

…conversation experienced a breakdown/breakthrough. Sound of a lone red blip marching across a dark mindscreen. Exegesis of telos. An infinite regression of flipflops preceded an endless precession of theses and antitheses… Theophany. Timecrashes and stickfigures and posthuman subterfuge…God said: There Is No Posthuman. Humanity Has Been Defined By Technology Since The First Infinitely Hot & Dense Nucleosyntheschiz. There Is Low Technology & There Is High Technology. Now Fuck Off…counterthesis…not enough secondary sources. Not enough graphic fornication. I cannot play to Infinity. My arm hangs from my torso like tenderized London Broil, torn and bloody, gnawed on by a rogue mammal. The other arm is gone. Vanished. Vaporized. In its place: a cone of ekphrasis wrapped in chickenwire…What came first, the beard or the high forehead? One of them will have to testify for the defense in the case of Brown vs. the Board of Technomasculine Desire…Dance sequence. Lavish description here set to a dull synthesizer…No matter what one does, no matter where one goes, one accomplishes the terminus of the same acronym: BFD (Big Fucking Deal). This is the price one must pay for the growlhound of narrative. Narrative extends from Donovan's Brain throughout the universe, tethered to the fiery assholes of insect-shaped spaceships…Media technologies explode implode explode etc. Big Bang Big Crunch etc. A boy stands alone on a beach. His mother died in a bugswarm. He hangs his head. The surf splashes onto his feet. It's quiet. He can't comprehend it. He imagines the Unnamable. He hears the theme song for Super Mario Bros. The sun claps off like a floodlight.

Fistfight. Orgasm.

It ended there. With a period. BFD.

Two minutes passed.

"Sid" said, "I have a picture. A photograph." He opened a wallet and removed an old, crinkled Polaroid. He studied it for a moment, then gave it to the doktor. "Take it. Look at it."

This is what Dr. Gradgrind saw:

He nodded and gave the Polaroid back to "Sid." "Sid" put it away. "It keeps appearing in my wallet," he admitted. "Every time I find it, I throw it in the garbage. Then I find it in my wallet again."

"Curious. Who is it?"

"I don't know. Me? I don't know. I think—"

Dr. Gradgrind tapped his watch and cleared his throat. "Let me stop youuuuuuuuuuu…just a moment……………just a moment………………… right…*there*."

Pause. "Ok," said "Sid."

"Our time is up for today," said Dr. Gradgrind.

Pause. "Ok."

"Let's pursue the matter of the photograph next time. 'The Photograph Matter,' as it were."

Pause. "Ok."

"Remember to take your medication."

Pause. "Ok."

"Sometimes the effekts aren't noticeable for years."

Pause. "Ok."

"I called your pharmacist personally and told him to give you an unlimited number of refills."

Pause. "Ok."

"No more than twelve milligrams a day."

Pause. "Ok."

"Take it easy, 'Sid.'"

Pause. "Ok."

"I'm serious. You need to relax."

Pause. "Ok."

"Smell the flowers and so forth. Try not to be an asshole. You know."

Pause. "Ok."

"And remember what I told you. Remember what I always tell you. You are not special or unique. But you exist. Somehow existence must be enough."

Pause. "Ok."

"Well. The session is over. You can leave now."

Pause. "Ok."

"You know where the door is."

Pause. "Ok."

"Goodbye."

Pause. "Goodbye."

It was the 257th time he turned into Kyoto.

十二

the 500th time I turned into kyoto

HAIKU + PROLOGUE + ETC. + HAIKU

a man's silhouette

flickers in the window—

the offal of God

Kyoto lies upon the earth like a sleeping dog. Overhead, the rays of a crimson sun bleed into an azure sky. No wind. Sound of a peacock spreading its tailfeathers...

Nobody practices tai chi near gardens of water and fragrance. Nobody wears thin-skinned gees and aerobicizes limbs in fluid, mechanical synch as a bird lands on the freshly pruned branch of a bonsai tree. Nobody inhales molecules and exhales fumes. Men in dreadnought coats are as much a mystery as they are nonentities.

Regiments of multicolored felt streamers and banners run vertically over the streets and hang down the faces of buildings. They are marked by thousands of golden Japanese symbols and icons in possession of deliberately cryptic meanings. Cobblestone streets. Green awnings. All of the zaibatsus have been consigned to an epistemological vacuum.

Difficult to gauge which Kyoto is this Kyoto. Kyoto present, past or future. Kyoto fact or fiction...

There is no time...The present does not exist—the moment it happens, it becomes the past. The future does not exist—the moment it becomes the present is the moment the present becomes the past. The past does not exist—prove it.

I can prove what I see now. Transparent eyeballs are for robosapiens in legwarmers. This is my prologue. It begins with a haiku. It ends with a haiku:

like the flower,

my petals rev and spin

like the turbine

The accidental tourist may dive off of any plateau and enter Kyoto from any orifice at any given time. No matter where you originate, you will culminate in the city.

This is not a movie. *Ceci n'est pas une image mobile.*

Evening. This sky is cobalt blue and swells of foliage glow red and orange and green and the golden spires of temples rise out of the foliage as if authorizing the science fictionalization of reality. Here is a picture:

Here is another picture:

IMAGE OF A CITY REPRESENTED BY THE FOLLOWING HAIKU:
a *metoroporisu* darkly
illuminated by strange fingers;
electric desolation…

Daimonji (大文字).

Wind kicks up. It echoes with the distant clang of swords, the erudite grunts of dead warriors.

Long, kinked filmstrip of Kyoto, each frame an Art Deco stillshot.

Creak of an opening book…

…gate of the Three Luminaries…a bamboo grove in the Sagano district…the moss garden at the temple Saiho-ji…sand cones erected on……painted statue of a geisha with hair ornament standing next to plum blossoms…Kung Fu studios constituted by sliding paper walls, restaurants constituted by sliding paper walls, living rooms constituted by sliding paper walls...the Shaka triad of Horyu-ji...expansion/clarification: the statue of the geisha possesses/professes multiple arms with stunted fingers; it may not be a geisha...

The moon hangs in a starless night sky like a shark tooth.

449 fathoms of
urban fles©h/ettes—
a quiet stain

十三

the sixth time i turned into kyoto

FLASH FICTION

...Adam's apple goes up and down and down goes eight milligrams of RX#4470973.

It was the 510th time I turned into Kyoto.

十四
the xxxth time I turned into kyoto
CHARACTER SKETCHES

INFODUMP, OR, THY PILES

In this chapter, a large number of "urban planners" or "social economists" or "joystick analysts" congregates at Camp Bell in Bliptown circa 2013 AR (After Reality) in order to discuss the most effektive means of negotiating the continued aggression of the Kyoto Man, who is systematically destroying the Earth. Describe each character in unbearable detail (approx. 4000 words apiece). Use ellipses *ad infinitum, per omnia saecula saeculorum*…Employ the following criteria:

NAME:

PHYSIOLOGY:

PHYSIOGNOMY:

PSYCHOLOGY:

PATHOLOGY:

PHRENOLOGY:

PHENOMENOLOGY:

NIKTO:

Halfway through the sketch of the twenty-sixth character, the Kyoto Man erupts somewhere nearby, razing Bliptown, and all of the "urban planners" or "social economists" or "joystick analysts" explode and burn. Emphasis on the whining futility of existence, the purring meaninglessness of life in postmediatized, postreal society, where the diegesis of a pop song dictates Any Which Way But Loose. Favor extrapolation over promulgation…[For the last sentence, do something different than the usual: "It was the xxxth time, etc."]

十五

the 666th time i turned into kyoto

FAIRY TALE

Once upon a timecrash there was a bounty hunter named Cyrano Nightranger. Mr. Nightranger had been commissioned by the Frogs of Industry to detain a man, dead or alive, who could metamorphose into a city. The name of this man was a subject of clambaked debate—different hermeneutics of suspicion revealed different signifiers.

INFODUMP, OR, THY PILES

To date, TKM (The Kyoto Man) had metamorphosed into the city on 665 isolated occasions/occlusions. The planet was in shambles. The infrastructure of the human mindscreen had collapsed like a haphazardly erected Tinkertoy. It had been determined by a well-respected TKTM (Tartar of the Kakistocracy of Telepathic Murnausferatu) that, if TKM metamorphosed on just one more occasion/occlusion, humanity would recede into the night. Cities could not be rebuilt at the rate he destroyed them. Even futuristic construction machinery failed to rally against his corporeal→architectonic prowess. Ancients and medievalites were completely helpless and could only administer blank stares if they survived the rude Armageddon. Wind blew harder in the absence of Edifice, earthly or manmade. One myth recounts that, as a goodwill effort, TKM attempted to follow in Frankenstein's monster's footsteps and retreat to the Arctic, via the Orkney Islands [beat] Iceland [beat] Greenland, where he could no longer harrow the human race with the threat of extinction. But the deep cold winters prompted rabid transformations from man to metropolis, the friction of which melted the polar ice caps...Canada was gone. Michigan was gone. And yet Michiganders had always been Canadians at heart, despite being associated with Midwestern Amerikan ethics, ideologies, *modes de vie*, etc....

The question remains as to how we arrived at a figure of 665 occasions/occlusions. Such a transformation is no doubt difficult if not impossible to document and historicize. Even TKM himself claimed not to know how many times he had "behaved badly," as he framed it in an interview on the Red Sky at Morning Show with Kalypso Shadrach, although, *ad infinitum*, *per omnia saecula saeculorum*, whether or not this man was the man who had "behaved badly" could not be proven by apposite kakistocratic personnel. In any event, the number 665 was decided upon by the very TKTM who concluded/ occluded that a 666th metamorphosis would incite a global apocalypse. The board members knew well that 666 was the mark of Satan, but they made no attempt to correlate TKM's antics with devilry—Biblical, literary, filmic, etc.—chalking up the matter to AFC (Absolute Fucking Coincidence). AFC, after all, had been responsible for some of history's greatest horrors, e.g., the circumstances that led to the rise of Adolph Hitler and the Third Reich. Hitler was cited on countless occasions/ occlusions by TKTM in defense of the argument to the point that we began to doubt if Hitler even existed in the first place, let alone TKTM, who could not exist in any case as clairvoyance is the stuff of dreams, insofar as we can remember what historical artifacts such as dreams "look like"...

The fairy tale bursts at the seams, rupturing into the Ordinary.

...slipped into a burnt sienna knee-length leather jacket, vintage, circa 1970s, with a jackknife collar and roomy sleeves that fell below the wrist. Mr.

Nightranger called the act of putting on the jacket a "brownout" in view of how it jeopardized his archetypal all-black image. But he remained black enough, and a little variety *dans le modèle* had never been anyone's death-knell. It was at this juncture that he developed a troubling relationship with eggs. He could not describe the relationship. Likewise he could not deny the relationship.

TCZ.

Mr. Nightranger no longer wore the brown leather jacket but the skin of a lion; the dead animal's jaw fit nicely on his skull, fangs snug against the temples. He shrugged the skin off and surveyed his outfit. Same all-black ensemble he had put on before Time and Space had burst like an amniotic sac of ignited hydrogen sulfide.

Vertigo. False memories of soul murder...

A red room. On one wall hung a landscape portrait of Bavarian mountains — profound snow-capped peaks overlooked a valley, green and sloping, that rolled into a smooth blue tarn; in the distance, a castle rose from the trees like a cluster of white rockets. There was a porcelain sink in the corner, and next to it a children's desk, with a long, slender book neatly arranged on its surface.

Naked and shaved, the twins hung on meathooks attached to cables that rose to the ceiling.

They were boys. Eyes closed. Skin pallid, unblemished.

Their toes grazed back and forth across small pools of blood that had accumulated on the floortile beneath them.

Mr. Nightranger shuddered...felt something cold and anomalous...another false memory. The abductor spoke through the medium of the abducted, his mouth a deflated gash...

He turned his head. A tombstone scraped against bedrock...

A man. Nondescript. And yet not without character. Tall, thin, neat. He wore a blue uniform and hat that looked more like a Halloween costume than an authentic emblem of professionalism. His eyes were steel gray, with red irises, the walls producing a photographic effekt.

The nametag on his chest read:

MR. WHITE

"Who are you?" asked Mr. Nightranger. His voice reverberated like a dull electric charge.

Mr. White said, "I don't know."

"Where are we?" Mr. Nightranger's hands grew heavy, as if filling with sand. His fingertips turned purple and exploded like haywire coronets...The mindscreen played and rewound and replayed the scene—an act of imagination against his will.

"Where are we?" he repeated.

Mr. White said, "The nightmare of reality. The panic room of narrative."

Vertigo. Mnemonic fictions...

A figure entered the room through a faux portal, head obfuscated by a nimbus cloud. Sturdy puffs emerged from the cloud near the mouth region, then ascended and spread across the ceiling in a poetic succession of ripples. A white jacket fell from the cloud like a curtain, tethered at the waist. The figure carried a black case. Its shoulders arched from its torso like cannonballs on sticks of bamboo.

Mr. Nightranger and Mr. White stared absently at the figure as it drifted across the room toward the twins.

The smoke cleared as the figure placed the case on the edge of the sink, turned on the faucet, and doused the arm of a monstrous smoking instrument, something like a cigar, or a bong, but more complex, its bulk technologized by a trellis of slim tubes and copper wires.

Full head of gleaming black hair. Rounded jaw. Pejorative rictus grin.

Dr. Josef Mengele.

[Halfway across the sky, we hear the tsunamic curses of **Ira Überstein**.]

He brushed off his hands and lit a cigarette. He smoked it to the filter with Olympic velocity and lit another one, smoking it slower, relishing it, lips treating the butt like hard candy, sucking it, milking it, salivating on it...

Chainsmoking, Dr. Mengele snapped on surgical gloves. He removed a scalpel from the case.

He made an insertion into one of the twins' abdomens.

The twin's eyes opened, flared...He screamed. At first he didn't know why. His brother jolted awake. Screamed...They groped and writhed on the meathooks.

Dr. Mengele punched the twins in the heads, dazing them, and then he shoved a fist into the new wound. He probed the region, dreams of history slipping through his fingers...He seized the artifact. Cigarette clenched between twisted incisors, he removed his hand, gripping what appeared to be a tract of barbed wire, jointed like a chainlink, wet with dark purple blood and bright yellow bits of tissue. "Hand über Faust," he announced...Each barb became progressively larger and opened the wound wider as it came out and the twins screamed louder and louder...Dr. Mengele accelerated the process, as if taking up an anchor from a boat, and the wire went on and on and on and formed a pile of metal and gore at the doktor's feet as the hysterical twin collapsed and crumpled, desiccated, skin wrinkling, legs and arms disappearing into his torso.

The last barb to emerge from the twin was the size of a billiard. The twin twitched obscenely, drooling and blubbering. Then he wilted, died. The soaking husk of a junebug.

Dr. Mengele silenced the brother with another punch, cracking the boy's neck.

The twins' corpses quietly swung back and forth on the meathooks.

Mr. Nightranger and Mr. White monitored the *conte cruel* idly, with detached awareness. They felt next to nothing yet were perfectly aware of the circumstances.

They couldn't move. Awake, alive, but numb—they had slipped into a trancelike state. Neither man knew when it began. Mr. Nightranger worried that it would never end.

Dr. Mengele peeled off the gloves and dropped them into the sink. He crushed out a cigarette with his boot heel and lit another one.

He turned and caught his breath, glaring down at the intruders.

"Der Poisoner aller Nationen," he said automatically. A subtitle in crisp white lettering formed beneath his feet: "THE POISONER OF ALL NATIONS."

Either the doktor's gaze or the sound of his voice dissolved the spell—Mr. Nightranger and Mr. White were free.

"Mengele," said Mr. White. "I know you. I killed you."

The doktor laughed. "ABSURD," read the subtitles. "I AM NOT DEAD. I AM ALIVE. I WILL ALWAYS BE ALIVE."

"What's happening?" said Mr. Nightranger.

Mr. White removed his hat and tucked it beneath an armpit, as if preparing to deliver a business pitch. "Calm down. I'll handle this." He stepped towards Dr. Mengele.

"GAAAAAAAURDS!!!" read the subtitle.

"Nobody's coming," said Mr. White. "It's me and you, Herr Doktor. I killed you before. I'll kill you again. No matter how many times I find you, I'll kill you. Because Time and Space want me to."

Terrified, Dr. Mengele paced backwards. He was four feet taller than the stranger and carried 200+ more pounds of lean muscle. Tolerably versed in the English language, he got the drift of what Mr. White had said to him; meaning-making was another matter. He had certainly never seen Mr. White before. But something about the man touched a nerve in his core. The immanence of his own death overwhelmed him. He hyperventilated.

PANTING SOUNDS, read the subtitles.

Mr. White moved forward. "Grow up, meathead. If you want to be a crazy Nazi pimp, you must be prepared to look long into the abyss."

"What's happening?" said Mr. Nightranger.

Dr. Mengele fell to his knees—slow splash of blood—and broke into tears. He continued to chainsmoke.

WEEP. PUFFPUFFPUFFPUFF. WEEP, WEEP.

AIIEEE![1]

Mr. Nightranger stood agape.

Mr. White slapped him. "Snap out of it. You're having a breakdown. You've been standing there for hours. You're not breathing."

Rubbing his jaw, Mr. Nightranger thanked him for saving his life. They drifted into a heated discussion about eggs—cooking techniques, symbolic

---

1   According to *KA-BOOM!: A Dictionary of Comic Book Words, Symbols & Onomatopoeia*, self-published by Kevin Taylor, this expression denotes "a cry of anguish, fear, pain, etc." (10).

applications, the emergence from the cloaca, etc.—and concluded that the subject of the conversation was, while riveting, ultimately pedestrian. They moved on to other topics, territorializing with one word what they deterritorialized with another, as dark human effigies flickered in and out of view, menacing shadows and silhouettes, creatures of intelligent civilization...

The room filled with the traffic of existence.

Oblivion.

Mr. Nightranger blinked. "Where did everybody go?"

"I don't know." A history of carnage retreated to the far corners of Mr. White's mindscreen.

Even the corpses of Dr. Mengele and the twins were gone. And the room had been cleaned, sanitized. "Something's wrong. We need something." He cogitated. "Exposition. Infodump. Thy piles..."

"What's that?" Mr. Nightranger raised an arm and pointed at the desk. He kept his arm extended as he walked over to it. Mr. White joined him.

Shoulder to shoulder, they stared down at the book. It was a children's book. The title:

The Awful Boy Who Turned into an Even Awfuler Man
by
Stanley Ashenbach

And for its cover art, an illustrated black-and-white version of this picture:

"That looks like somebody," said Mr. Nightranger.

Mr. White coughed. "Everybody looks like somebody." He reached down and opened the cover to the first page in the center of which was a quote.

"No man is an island. But one man is a city."
—Jean-Jacques Faitremonté

"What's that mean?" said Mr. Nightranger.

"I don't know," said Mr. White.

"Who's Jean-Jacques Fatermont?"

"Faitremonté."

"Right. Fatermont."

"I don't know."

They listened to each other breathe. Mr. White turned the page. There was a dedication. It read:

I dedicate this shitty book to whoever wants it. It is the first and last goddamn book I will ever write. Sayonara. If anybody needs me, I will be in the weight room getting jacked. Fuck off.

Mr. Nightranger made a face. "That's no way to act. What kind of dedication is that?"

"I don't know." Mr. White turned the page, paused, and turned the page again. He continued in this fashion until he reached PAGE 42...

The plot unfolded with minimalist efficacy. On each page, a boy stared at the readers—the same boy on the cover of the book—standing straight, arms limp, feet shoulder width apart, sometimes blank-faced, sometimes expressing emotion, but never a surplus of emotion, and always making the readers feel uncomfortable, somehow, implicating them for something they had done or were about to do. There was no writing. No dialogue, no descriptive passages. No exegeses. The boy told the story with his face, his posture.

He got older. Taller. Mr. Nightranger and Mr. White watched him pass through the awkwardness of puberty and then his jaw sharpened and his limbs filled out and he grew a flimsy goatee and it disappeared and he grew a thick mustache and it disappeared and then Mr. Nightranger looked back and forth between the book and Mr. White and the book and Mr. White and so on and wild-eyed he said:

"It's you."

Turning the pages with increasing urgency, Mr. White said, "It's me."

On PAGE 42, Mr. White began to metamorphose into a city...

The scene slipped into slow motion as Mr. Nightranger produced a weapon. "You're coming with me," he said in a deep, languid drawl.

On PAGE 44, flesh gave way to WOOD-REEDS-PLANKS.

The walls of the red room broke like pulp. Mr. Nightranger slipped through the jagged interstices.

On PAGE 46, WOOD-REEDS-PLANKS conquered flesh. Usurpers.

The walls opened up like vortexes, consuming Mr. Nightranger. One wall after another. He fell into eternity again and again and again.

On PAGE 49, a city slept beneath a red sun.

Image of Mr. Nightranger treading the black, vacuous waters of the Outer Limits. He held his breath, placing his thoughts elsewhere. He didn't fear death. What frightened him was life.

On PAGE 50, centered: "It was the 666th time he turned into Kyoto."

十六

the 666th time ı turned into kyoto

SCRIPT FOR COMIC BOOK

(ADAPTED FROM THE FAIRY TALE THAT FAILED)

PAGE 1 - 6 PANELS

[1]-[6]   BEGIN WITH **CLOSEUP** ON THE HAZY SILHOUETTE OF
           A JAPANESE CITY. RED-ORANGE SKY. EACH SUBSE-
           QUENT PANEL **ZOOMS OUT**. WE SEE THAT THE CITY
           APPEARS ON A VINTAGE HOFFMAN TELEVISION SET
           SURROUNDED BY GALAXIES OF STATIC/STARS.

PAGE 2 - 6 PANELS

[1]-[4]   THE CITY COAGULATES INTO AN IRIS AND THE TELE-
           VISION SET MELTS INTO A GLINTING MANGA EYE.

[5]-[6]   **POV PULLS BACK** TO REVEAL THE PARTIAL FACE OF
           MR. WHITE.

PAGE 3 - 1 PANEL

[1]   **UPPER BODY SHOT** OF **MR. WHITE**. HE LOOKS LIKE
           AN OLDER VERSION OF DEREK WILDSTAR IN THE
           AMERIKAN ANIMÉ TELEVISION SERIES *STAR BLAZ-
           ERS* — BUSHY BROWN HAIR, THICK BROWN EYE-
           BROWS, NUBBED NOSE, VAGUE CHEEKBONES, LIP-
           LESS, BUT ATTRACTIVE — ONLY INSTEAD OF A
           STARSHIP ARGO UNIFORM HE WEARS A MAYTAG MAN
           UNIFORM. CONFUSED, INTENSE EXPRESSION. HE
           APPEARS AT ONCE ON THE VERGE OF SEXUAL CLI-
           MAX AND COLLAPSE INTO PARANORMAL APATHY.

PAGE 4 - 6 PANELS

[1]   **WIDER SHOT. MR. WHITE** STANDS NEXT TO ANOTHER

MAN, **MR. NIGHTRANGER**. BOTH STARE BLANKLY AT
THE READER. **MR. NIGHTRANGER** IS A MANGATIZED
VERSION OF GIL GERARD IN *BUCK ROGERS IN THE
TWENTY-FIFTH CENTURY* — NEATLY COMBED BROWN
HAIR, TRIM SIDEBURNS, BLUE EYES, STRONG
NOSE, SQUARE CHIN — DEVASTATINGLY HANDSOME
IN A RETROFUTURISTIC WAY, AND YET SOMETHING
ABOUT HIS FACE SUGGESTS A FAT MAN WAITING
TO BREAK FREE. ADDITIONALLY, INSTEAD OF A
SPANDEX WHITE DEFENSE DIRECTORATE UNIFORM,
HE WEARS THE SKIN OF A LION; THE DEAD ANI-
MAL'S JAW FITS NICELY ON HIS HEAD, FANGS
SNUG AGAINST THE TEMPLES.

[2]-[4]   REPEAT [1].

[5]   REPEAT [1], ONLY **MR. NIGHTRANGER** IS GRIMAC-
           ING.

[6]   REPEAT [1], ONLY **MR. NIGHTRANGER** HAS SHRUGGED
           OFF THE LION SKIN. HE WEARS AN ALL-BLACK FU-
           TURISTIC COWBOY COSTUME À LA YUL BRYNNER IN
           WESTWORLD.

PAGE 5 — 98 PANELS

[1]   **REVERSE POV - WIDE VIEW** OF THE ROOM. TWO
           NAKED **TWIN BOYS** SANS NIPPLES AND GENITALS
           HANG FROM MEATHOOKS ATTACHED TO CABLES THAT
           RISE INTO THE CEILING. EYES CLOSED, HEADS
           SLUMPED ONTO SHOULDERS. BLOOD DRIPS OFF OF
           THEIR TOES FROM UNSEEN WOUNDS, FORMING NEAT
           POOLS BENEATH THEM. TO THE RIGHT IS A SMALL
           ELEMENTARY SCHOOL DESK AND CHAIR, TO THE
           LEFT A SINK AND COUNTER.

[2]   **FULL SHOT** OF **TWINS - CLOSER.**

[3]   **HEAD SHOT** OF **TWINS**.

[4]-[95]   **FULL SHOT** OF **MR. WHITE** AND **MR. NIGHTRANGER**.

[96]   REPEAT [96].

Mr. Nightranger: WHERE *ARE* WE?

[97]   REPEAT [4]-[95].

[98]   REPEAT [97].

Mr. White: THE NIGHTMARE OF REALITY.

PAGE 6 - 2 PANELS

PAGE SPLIT IN TWO BY A CRACK THAT RUNS FROM THE UPPER
RIGHT CORNER TO THE LOWER LEFT CORNER.

[1]   MIRRORED BACKGROUND.

           Title: *THE NIGHTMARE OF REALITY!!!*

[2]   BLACK BACKGROUND. MANGATIZED **STILL SHOT** OF A
           YOUNG GLEN CAMPBELL SINGING "WICHITA LINEMAN"
           ON THE SMOTHERS BROTHERS SHOW CIRCA 1969.

PAGE 7 - 4 PANELS

[1]   **OBLIQUE SHOT** OF A BLANK WALL - **POV** VIA THE
           CORNERS OF **MR. WHITE**'S EYES.

[2]-[3]   A DOOR FORMS IN THE WALL.

[4]   THE DOOR OPENS.

           Caption: *K-K-KREEAK!!!*

FLOATING PANEL

HEAD SHOT OF **MR. WHITE**. HIS FACE HAS BEEN ERASED. THIS PANEL PENETRATES NARRATIVE SPACETIME *DE RI-GUEUR*, OOZING ACROSS THE PAGES OF THE COMIC LIKE AN AMOEBA.

PAGE 8 - 7 PANELS

[1]   **HEAD SHOT** OF A STONE-FACED **MR. WHITE**.

[2]   **HEAD SHOT** OF A CONFUSED-LOOKING **MR. NIGHT-RANGER**.

[3]   VIEW OF THE OPEN DOOR. WE CAN'T SEE ANYTHING INSIDE (REF. THE ORIGINAL COVER ART FOR KAFKA'S *THE METAMORPHOSIS*).

[4]-[7]   A GIANT ENTERS/EXITS THE DOOR. THIS IS **DR. MENGELE**. PROTOTYPE: JAWS (PERF. RICHARD KIEL) FROM *MOONRAKER*. HE WEARS A CLOAK OF GREEN SCALES BOUND TIGHTLY AT THE NECK AND SMOKES GAULOISES, THE BRAND OF JEAN-PAUL SARTRE. HE WALKS ACROSS THE ROOM TO THE TWINS.

PAGE 9 - 10 PANELS

IN EACH PANEL, **DR. MENGELE** PUNCHES THE TWINS, ONE AFTER THE OTHER, ALTERNATING BETWEEN BLOWS TO THE FACE AND TORSO. THEY DON'T WAKE UP. EACH PUNCH PRODUCES A DIFFERENT ONOMATOPOEIAC REPORT.

[1]   Caption: *KAA-POW!*

[2]   Caption: *PAFF!*

[3]   Caption: *TCHUNK!*

[4]   Caption: *KLUDD!*

[5]   Caption: *THUK!*

[6]   Caption: *FRUNK!*

[7]   Caption: *WHPSH!*

[8]   Caption: *THWAPP!*

[9]   Caption: *BLIKX!*

[10]   ANIMATED PANEL. PANTING, **DR. MENGELE** FIN-
             ISHES HIS CIGARETTE AND LIGHTS ANOTHER. HE
             SMOKES IT AS FAST AS HE CAN. HE SMOKES AN-
             OTHER ONE EVEN FASTER. HE CONTINUES IN THIS
             FASION UNTIL HIS BREATHING RETURNS TO NOR-
             MAL. THEN THE PANEL REBOOTS.

PAGE 10 - 1 PANEL

[1]   **CLOSE** ON **MR. WHITE**. A FANATIC DELIRIUM MARKS
             HIS EYES, LIKE A STRANDED ESKIMO, NOTHING
             BUT MAN AND SNOW AND SPACE AND SKY.

T-Bubble: I *KNOW* SOMETHING ISN'T RIGHT. THIS DIDN'T *HAPPEN* IN THE BOOK. I
             DON'T KNOW WHAT *BOOK* I MEAN, BUT I *KNOW* SOMETHING ABOUT A
             BOOK, AND I *KNOW* IT DIDN'T *HAPPEN* THERE. *SOMETHING* IS *HAPPENING.*

PAGE 11 - 2 PANELS

[1]   SHOT OF **MR. WHITE** AND **MR. NIGHTRANGER** FROM
             THE CEILING. WE SEE THAT MR. WHITE'S HAT HAS
             A CRYPTIC JAPANESE SYMBOL ON IT AND THAT MR.
             NIGHTRANGER HAS AN INTRUSIVE BALD SPOT.

Mr. Nightranger: I CAN'T *MOVE.*

[2]   REVERSE ANGLE FROM [1], ON THE FLOOR, LOOK-
             ING UP AT A SET OF CLEANLY SHAVEN CHINS.

Mr. White: WE'RE NOT *SUPPOSED* TO MOVE. *ANYTHING* CAN *HAPPEN.*

PAGE 12 - 12 PANELS

[1]-[12]   SUBLIMINAL FLASHBULB SEQUENCE, WITH ODD PAN-
             ELS IN THE OUTLINE OF A SLEEPING FETUS AND
             EVEN PANELS SHAPED LIKE BANAL TWO-DIMENSIONAL
             EXPLOSIONS. WE ARE PRESENTED WITH A **SERIES OF
             STILL AND ANIMATED IMAGES** THAT BELONG TO THE
             UNCONSIOUSNESS OF ONE OR MORE OF THE CHARAC-
             TERS. WE CAN'T BE CERTAIN WHICH CHARACTER(S)
             PRODUCED WHICH IMAGE(S). A MAN WITH A GOAT
             HEAD RECURS IN THREE OF THE PANELS, ONCE IN
             THE FOREGROUND, TWICE IN THE BACKGROUND. ONE
             PANEL CONTAINS A CRACKED, BLEEDING TELEVISION
             SET AGAINST A CANVAS OF STATIC/SPACE (REF.
             PG. 1). ANOTHER CONTAINS A NIGHT TERROR SO
             GRAPHIC AND HIDEOUS IT CAN ONLY BE ARTICU-
             LATED IN ILLUSTRATED FORM.

PAGE 13 - 6 PANELS

[1]   IN THE REAL WORLD, PIGEONS ATTACK THE FARM-
             HOUSE OF HUMAN DISTINCTION WITH RENEWED ACRI-
             MONY. THE CLOUDS THREATEN TO EXCRETE TORNA-
             DOES, DARK AND PHALLIC CONDUITS REACHING FOR
             THE EARTH. THE AMERIKAN PEOPLE ARE INTELLIGENT
             AND FEAR ALL SYMPTOMS OF ABLATION. GRATUITOUS
             BEAVER SHOT — IT ENGULFS THE PANEL AND IN-
             TOXICATES THE BLOODSTREAM. IDAHO. WHAT NEXT? A
             SHIPWRECK? THE *S.S. BUZZARDSPOON* CRASHES INTO
             A TOWERING ISLAND REEF GOING 100 CPH. BAR TEN-
             DERS, LOUNGE SINGERS, LICENSED MARINERS, NAVY
             SEALS, SMOKESTACK SWEEPERS FLY OFF THE DECK
             AND ARE IMPALED ON A VAST, OTHERWORLDLY BED

OF STALAGMITES. DEATH THROES. TRIBUTARIES OF
BLOOD. NATIVE ISLANDERS SWARM THE CARNAGE LIKE
TERMITES. COLONIALISTS MUST BE TAUGHT A LES-
SON. APOCALYPTIC MACHETES. A KRAKEN RISES
FROM THE SURF AND DEVOURS THE NATIVES BY
THE HANDFUL. SOPWITH CAMEL WARPLANES SPUTTER
OVERHEAD AND DROP BOMBS THE SIZE OF MULES.
PYROTECHNICS. MORE MACHETES. A WARPLANE FLIES
INTO THE KRAKEN'S CYCLOPTIC EYE AND THE SEA
MONSTER TOPPLES OVER WITH A RESOUNDING GRUNT.
ACROSS THE UNIVERSE A METEOR SPIRALS INTO A
BLACK HOLE. ON THE OTHER SIDE OF THE ISLAND
ANOTHER SHIP, THE *S.S. YANOMAMO*, CRASHES. NO
STALAGMITES HERE. NO BOULDERS OR ROCKS. ONLY
A SMOOTH WHITE COASTLINE — AND YET THE *S.S.
YANOMAMO* STILL, BY HOOK OR BY CROOK, CRASHES.
EVERY SOUL ON BOARD SURVIVES. THEY DASH TO
THE ISLAND'S HIGHEST PEAK AND ERECT A CHURCH
WITH STEEPLES AND BELL TOWERS AND GARGOYLES
AND THE PASTOR SLAMS HIS FIST ONTO THE LECTERN,
BREAKING IT IN HALF LIKE A STACK OF CINDER-
BLOCKS. THE CONGREGATION RESPONDS IN TONGUES
AND PUTS ON CAPES, THE COLLARS OF WHICH SWAL-
LOW THEIR HEADS. IN THE VESTIBULE, CHILDREN
PLAY WITH ANTIQUE RUBBER AND CAST-IRON TOYS.
IN THE BELFRY, AN ARTHRITIC HUNCHBACK SWINGS
ON A BELL CLAPPER LIKE A MONKEY. IN THE BASE-
MENT, A MAN SWALLOWS HIS MEDICATION AND WAITS,
PATIENTLY, FOR THE PAIN TO SUBSIDE.

[2]-[6]   DR. MENGELE FIRES UP A CHAINSAW AND STANDS
BEFORE HIS PREY LIKE A MOUNTAIN GOD, REVVING
THE MACHINE. THE TWINS WAKE UP IN PANEL [3].
THEY SCREAM FROM IMPROVISED MOUTHS.

Twins: *AAIIIEEEEE!!!*

THE EXCLAMATION OVERLAPS MULTIPLE PANELS.

PAGE 14 - 4 PANELS

[1]   **MR. NIGHTRANGER** LOOKS BEWILDERED HERE, SENS-
             ING THE PROXIMITY OF SOMETHING UNPLEASANT.
             NEXT TO HIM **MR. WHITE** YAWNS.

[2]+[4]   **MR. NIGHTRANGER** FALLS FROM PANEL [2] INTO
             PANEL [4] BENEATH IT...REFER TO NATSUME FU-
             SANOSUKE'S *MANGA GAKU: MANGA DE MANGA O YOMU*
             (1992) IN WHICH FRAMES CRACK AND RUPTURE AND
             CHARACTERS EXPLODE FROM ONE FRAME INTO AN-
             OTHER. NOTE THE FOLLOWING DIALOGUE SPOKEN BY
             THE META-MANGA'S PROTAGONIST:

             "THE USE OF FRAMES REALLY BEGINS TO OPEN NEW TERRITORY FOR
             EXPRESSION...ADD TO THIS A CINEMATIC APPROACH TO ANGLES AND
             EDITING, LEFT COMPLETELY TO THE READER'S IMAGINATION...[AND
             YET] IF THE FRAME SHOULD BECOME FLUID AND UNPREDICTABLE, THE
             SENSE OF REALITY GIVES WAY TO INSECURITY. AND IF THIS TECHNIQUE
             IS PUSHED TO EXTREMES, THE NARRATIVE COMPLETELY COLLAPSES."

             (**NOTE TO ILLUSTRATOR:** THE ABOVE DIALOGUE MUST
             NOT APPEAR IN THE ACTUAL COMIC. IT MUST EXIST
             ONLY IN THE MIND OF THE ARTIST WHO PRODUC-
             ES THE COMIC, INFLUENCING AND PATHOLOGIZING
             HIM, AND DENIED ALTOGETHER TO THE READER AT
             THE OTHER END OF THE TUNNEL.)

[3]   **MR. WHITE** REGARDS THE FALL OF **MR. NIGHT-
             RANGER** LIKE A CAR CRASH HAPPENING IN SLOW
             MOTION, GLANCING UP AT PANEL [2]. THERE IS
             A HOLE IN THE FLOOR BESIDE HIM.

PAGE 14 - 100,000 PANELS

[1]-
[99,000]   **MR. NIGHTRANGER** FINDS HIMSELF IN ANOTHER
             STERILE ROOM. INSTEAD OF TWINS HANGING FROM

> HOOKS, THERE IS A **WOMAN**, MILDLY ATTRACTIVE,
> WITH DIRTY BLONDE HAIR AND GOOD BONE STRUC-
> TURE. SHE WEARS A BUSINESS COAT AND SHORT
> SKIRT AND HER LEGS ARE HAIRY. **MR. NIGHT-
> RANGER** FALLS IN LOVE WITH HER. HE DOESN'T
> LIKE THE HAIRY LEGS AND WORRIES ABOUT THEM.
> NONETHELESS...AROUND PANEL [8000] OR [9000],
> SHE TELLS HIM HER NAME.

Woman: MY NAME IS DORA.

Mr. Nightranger: DORA. DORA...THAT SOUNDS MADE UP.

Woman: MY NAME IS DORA.

Mr. Nightranger: DORA. DORA...

> SUBSEQUENTLY THEY DEVELOP A RELATIONSHIP THAT
> OSCILLATES BETWEEN DEEP INTIMACY AND ILLOGI-
> CAL DETACHEDNESS. THEY FIGHT. THEY FUCK. THEY
> DINE. THEY TALK. SAMPLE DIALOGUE:

Mr. Nightranger: I AM *VERY* GOOD IN *BED*. THAT'S DIRECT MARKETING.

Woman: I HAVE A *VENEREAL DISEASE*.

Mr. Nightranger: UNFORTUNATELY THERE'S NO TIME FOR LOVE. I MUST CAPTURE THE *MAN→CITY*. HE'S GOING TO STOP THE EARTH FROM *REVOLVING*. DO YOU KNOW WHAT THAT WILL MEAN? AS SOON AS THE MOTION STOPS, ALL OF THE *PEOPLE* WILL FLY OFF OF THE EARTH INTO OUTER SPACE!

Woman: I DIDN'T MEAN WHAT I SAID ABOUT THE VENEREAL DISEASE. I DON'T HAVE ONE.

Mr. Nightranger: WILT THOU, WHOSE *WILL* IS LARGE AND SPACIOUS, NOT ONCE VOUCHSAFE TO HIDE MY *WILL* IN THINE?

Woman: I AM A *BORN-AGAIN* VIRGIN.

AND SO ON. THEY BREAK UP AND GET BACK TO-
GETHER AND BREAK UP AND GET BACK TOGETHER.
AND SO ON. THE FINAL, ANIMATED PANELS EMA-
NATE SOUND EFFEKTS TRIGGERED BY THE FLAT
GAZE OF THE READER. IN THEM, **MR. NIGHTRANGER**
AND THE **WOMAN** ENGAGE IN SOFTCORE PORNO AN-
TICS, MAKING OH-FACES, HAIR BLOWING IN THE
WIND OF TABLE FANS, HANDS AND CLOTHING CARE-
FULLY POSITIONED TO ENSURE THE VISUAL SUP-
PRESSION OF GENITALS. SOUND EFFEKTS RANGE
FROM DUBBED GERMAN UTTERANCES TO APROPOS
EROTIC RHAPSODIES.

[100,000] ANIMATED PANEL THE COLOR OF PRIMORDIAL SOUP.
IF THE READER STARES AT IT FOR MORE THAN
6.66 SECONDS, THE PANEL EXPLODES INTO A CITY
THAT ENGULFS THE REST OF THE COMIC.

PAGE 15 - 1 PANEL

[1]   STILL SHOT OF THE CITY OF KYOTO IN THE EDO
PERIOD (SEVENTEENTH CENTURY). THIS IS THE
ONLY COLOR IMAGE IN THE COMIC, THE REST OF
WHICH APPEARS IN HYPERSTYLIZED BLACK AND
CHROME BEFORE KYOTO DEVOURS IT.

Caption: IT WAS THE 666TH TIME HE TURNED INTO KYOTO.

THE END.

十七

the 666th time i turned into kyoto

COMIC BOOK PANEL

THE NIGHTMARE OF REALITY

十八

the 1000th time i turned into kyoto

**EXCERPT FROM *THE SLUTTY MINUTES: A NOVEL*,
ALLEGEDLY WRITTEN BY THE KYOTO MAN**

The manuscript for *The Slutty Minutes: A Novel* was discovered circa 2030 AD in an abandoned log cabin on the Cahulawassee River, which originates in Georgia's Blue Lick Mountains. Approximate date of composition: 1892 AD. It was composed by hand on a 100-foot roll of indissoluble alkaline papyrus. Harvard antiquarians, archivists, and holy divers claim the papyrus had been manufactured in the year 2189 AD and contained faint traces of Martian soil.

The following excerpt, "One Minute Before Dusk," constitutes the seventeenth of 306 chapters in *The Slutty Minutes: A Novel*. It is featured here with the permission of ASPRAEN (Amerikan Society for the Preservation of Recorded Acts of Evil Nihilism).

SEVENTEEN
One Minute Before Dusk

"*Mr. Smith Goes to Washington* is a VERY good movie," said Gregory Farnswürth, eyes crazed with purpose. "It's a Jimmy Stewart movie. I highly recommend it. You should see it. My church buddies and I just watched it the other day. Everybody liked it."

Ferdinand stared into space. "I've seen *Mr. Smith Goes to Washington*," he replied vacantly. "It was atrocious. One of the stupidest films I've ever watched. Lackluster. Plodding. *Stupid*. Jimmy Stewart is a douchebag. A bad actor with bad hair and a pedophilic accent. The man speaks with his teeth, not his tongue. Asshole. Cunt."

Taken aback, Gregory took a few moments to collect his wits. He had not expected such a brash and honest response. It was as if he had been hit in the chest with a rubber mallet. He felt hurt, violated. Confused. "You didn't like the movie?"

Ferdinand passed a blade across Gregory's throat, severing the trachea and jugular. Blood and mucous flowed down his sternum into his lap. Ambivalent, Gregory observed the gore, then turned his attention to Ferdinand. Before dying his mind wandered through a fresh world of morning. The sun peeked over a great willow tree on a golf course, showering his face with warmth.

Tomorrow, he thought. Tomorrow, tomorrow…

[With the exception of several flowery Rousseauesque passages, all of them disposable and in some instances abortive, the next 1509 words are unreadable, blotted with ink and, according to paleographic studies, tears and urine.]

…slut. She admitted it, too, after a share of unjust coaxing. And yet he didn't know how to negotiate this young lady's prehensile aggression. She hurled herself against the biological repercussion, ordered him to annul her, but as he adjusted the yoke, she distracted herself with postsynaptic alterity, etching slapdash glyphs into her turbocharged haecceity, and then she sacrificed herself to the dogpoets, dispensing with crotchwear and write-offs and qualia, and she demanded that he invalidate her, and when he adjusted the yoke a second time, she objectified him via references to the phalanges and the herpetologists and capricious focal adhesion, and she went on to emasculate him with an impressively diverse and well-seasoned lexicon of irreverence. Bitch. It was an unwarranted assault. He concluded that the human condition is at its worst in the delirium of machinic congress, even if congress isn't in session. The walls of civility fall away and we shit on etiquette, molesting our animal cores like anchoring fibrils. Performativity accompanies the locomotion.

From this point of departure, the would-be blacksmiths oscillated back and forth: one moment they exchanged tender apologies and compliments, the next they engaged in hot scatological martyrdoms. All orifices for themselves. She drifted into an ecstasy that transcended simple body-mindscreen pleasure, imagining a kind of galactic interpellation of her testimonial into the rotten mouths of scar gardens.

"I love you," he whispered. "I want to marry you. I want to spend my life with you and grow old together."

She made a face. "Grow old?" She made another face. "To grow old is to grow mold. There's nothing good about it, whether you do it alone, or among friends, or among humanity. I will always be young." She choked to death on a testimonial. "Now I am dead," were her dying words. Her breasts deflated and flopped into her armpits. Her lips twitched and wilted into an obscene denovation.

Wrinkled flower petals corkscrewed to the floor and congealed into a puddle of wet shit.

Ah, the slutty minutes...

He awoke, alone, supine, a bead of ejaculate hardened in his navel. Sunlight passed through a kinked blind. He winced, rolled over. Fell back asleep. Dreamt of forgotten memories, of equatorial humidity and Third World misery. Awoke, feeling refreshed. He stared at his forearm. The hair was getting longer and would have to be sheared. He wished he were different. A different person. With different desires, goals. "Dreams." It made him mad, this disability, this failure in his character for future change. He crawled out of bed. It was nearly dusk. He shuffled into the kitchen. Looked around, uncertain of his objective. He shuffled back to the bedroom and into the bathroom. He removed the ejaculate from his navel and dropped it in the sink and it clicked against the porcelain like a marble and disappeared into the drain. Stepping into the shower, he turned on a radio. The voice of **Travis Manderbean** said: "—sound and fury, signifying *everything*. Make no mistake, folks. When everything is signified, apocalypse ensues. The question is what kind of apocalypse. One in which a man named Ferdinand gazes at the dead rodents spread across the lawn? Or one that involves the junk props of the science fiction genre, a panoply of tentacled aliens, alternate histories, scheming androids, and gee-whiz hi-tech novums gone awry? Either way, the nuclear family will suffer. As in *The Parent Trap*. As in *The Sound of Music*, only in the end, the Nazis win, and the Von Trapps are hurled into a pit of fire. Recall *Where the Red Fern Grows*. The coonhounds die and are buried—that's life. If only every community would manufacture lifescapes that captured the evanescence of all things. This is the problem with humanity, dead or alive. The inoperable community. The fetid Norseman on the hilltop whose balls have gone unscrubbed for centuries. I am not trying to confuse you. I am merely the voice of representation in troubled times. Times have always been troubled. It doesn't get any better. And yet utopia is not out of reach. This is

Travis Manderbean. My real name is Travis Manderbean. Either I exist as a figment of one man's imagination, or I am a voice that echoes across the hills and valleys of every man and woman's auditory canal. Avoid stenosis; when the canals close, there's no going back. I own an original Picasso sketch called 'Pour Roby.' It is quite simple—chickenscratch, really. I suspect the artist produced it in a matter of seconds, perhaps while eating a poached egg for breakfast, or piddling around the *bagno*. In 1960, the sketch is worth 400 dollars. In 3060, it is worth one billion dollars. I will sell it to the tenth caller for this latter figure. If you are from the year 5070, you may just obtain the bargain of your life. This is Travis Manderbean. And now we return to the hyperkinetic gorefest—"

He stepped out of the shower and unplugged the radio. Drying off, sadness eclipsed madness. He knew he would always be the same. Neurons fired; terminal signals flowed down the snarl of wires. The sound of transformation wasn't meant for his ears. It fled across the crystal waters like the caw of an albatross.

十九

the 1001st time i turned into kyoto

HYPERKINETIC GOREFEST

A red sun blooms onto the white screen of sky / at the beginning of *the making of amerikans* g. stein inscribes "once an angry man dragged his father along the ground through his own orchard / 'stop!' cried the groaning old man at last / 'stop! I did not drag my father beyond this tree'" / thus she commences an attack on patriarchy and arboreality and goodoldboy networks of desire / the experience of reading this sycophantic book approaches soul murder / zeitgeists prefer the first stanza of "lunar baedeker" in which m. loy inscribes "a silver Lucifer / serves / cocaine in cornucopia" / notwithstanding that latter crag of alliteration, an always-already deranged slight of language / flashforward to the first words of *the artificial kid* / b. sterling inscribes "reverie shines, the planet's edge lined in luminous atmospheric haze, her broad, shallow seas sparkling, her big coral-atoll continents brown and green and white through rifts in scattered clouds" / a more authentic *techné* of text→subject conversion / and now we return to the hyperkinetic gorefest / timecrash timecrash timecrash timecrash zoneshift / *shogun assassin* (a.k.a. *kozure okami*) is an ultraviolent **jidaigeki** film tailormade for the Amerikan marketplace / released in 1980 / artisans of the samurai filmind regard it as a classic / it plumbs the transcendental depths and uncovers the bottom nature of evil chi and sckikungfi ethics / one should not possess (and be dis/possessed by) the audacity to inscribe a terminal paragraph (à la dostoevsky) / dostoevsky stands on the crenellated apex of the loftiest turret in debtors' prison / the author's silhouette looms like a Biblical plague above a flatland of stripmalls / of martial arts studios / of coffee shops / of oil quickchange stations / this is the future / the way of the future / and now we return to the hyperkinetic gorefest / kyoto is a city that lives in a van down by the river / i.e. a list of important **daikaiju** monsters incl. biollante (transforming plant monster) gezorah (giant alien-possessed cuttlefish) hedorah (pollution-spawned monster) spacegodzilla (mutated godzilla clone) dagora (carbon-consuming space monster) monster x (mysterious alien monster) / i.e. there is more to life than **daikaiju** and vicissitudes of flesh and edifice / timecrash zoneshift timecrash / a mantra rattles down the hallways of the white motel / THE SKY THE SURF THE WIND IN MY HAIR / THE SKY THE SURF THE WIND IN MY HAIR / christ if my love were in my arms and I in my bed again / and now we return to the hyperkinetic gorefest / infodump or thy piles / **the war had been fought by stick figures controlled from remote bird nests / it lasted for fifty years / in its wake urbanity disappeared / they tried to rebuild the cities but every time they imprinted a skyline onto the horizon it imploded and the earth swallowed the superstructure and the memory of creationism / time passed / eventually the humans that remained on earth forgot how to build things / etc.** / the aforementioned legend belongs to a secondary character named **ira überstein** and he loves **travis manderbean** / (they might be the same prestidigitator) / there's another secondary character who drags around a bench everywhere he goes because he's afraid to sit down on any inanimate object but the bench / however the central question regarding the main character and primary textual instrument remains / not only why he transforms into a city / why the city of kyoto japan / the answer to this question issues from the loudspeakers in the rafters of the pole barn / the answer reminisces a gramophone recording disrupted by eerie scratches skips blips / the answer succumbs to a war between sentient metropoli (à la *clash of the titans* vis-à-vis molting cities instead of mythological superhumans and gods and beasts) / antennas cross like swords / leaning towers collide / chunks of asphalt catapult across the sky in broad arcs and rubble bleeds into the gutters / and now we return to the hyperkinetic gorefest / in *the philosophy of time travel* r. sparrow inscribes "when a tangent universe occurs those living nearest to the vortex will find themselves at the epicenter of a dangerous new world" / and later r. sparrow inscribes "the manipulated living are often the close friends and neighbors of the living receiver they are prone to irrational bizarre and often violent behavior this is the unfortunate result of their task which is to assist the living receiver in returning the artifact to the primary universe the manipulated living will do anything to save themselves from oblivion" / truer words never spoken-stolen / this is not a movie / this is what happens when talking heads stop dreaming and reality becomes ubiquity / the kyoto man becomes an outréman and peregrinates from lifescape to lifescape ravaging the postapocalyptic mythemes épistèmes metonymies / tcz / temporal fashion catastrophe / long tears in the stockingfabric of the spacetime continuum render different spontaneous fashion statements and architectures all imploding and collapsing into one another / everybody hallucinates an alien-capitalist takeover from a control booth in the attic of the organic theater / the manuscript dies / fiction devolves into fact / alpha into omega / blankety blank / the rape of narrative etiquette / galactic anus of bad storytelling / ur-constructedness / destined to weird gradients / the retro(re)-creation of history / an ultraviolent affair / a hyperkinetic gorefest / timecrash timecrash / sickness jaundice metrometafictionalmorphosis / it is the 1001st time he turns into kyoto / and in the end everybody is born and lives and dies and is forgotten / there is only a zero degree of meaning / there is only _____ / there is only the sky / the surf / the wind in my hair...

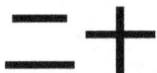

the zoooth time i turned into kyoto

SCRIPT FOR ADVERTISEMENT IN HOMEOPAPE

VIDEO	AUDIO
PANORAMA-CHIC IMAGE OF PRIMORDIAL SOUP.	Deep, rumbling voice, like the voice of a vengeful god, or a heavy smoker with a bad cold: "I lost trillions of pounds!"
FLASHCUT TO BIRDSEYE VIEW OF A CITY. PANNING. FEATURES INCL. BUDDHIST TEMPLES, SHINTO SHRINES AND TEAHOUSES GARNISHED WITH WEEPING WILLOW, TAKAO MAPLE AND KATSURA TREES. OCASSIONALLY A MIRRORED SKYSCRAPER INTERRUPTS THE STRUCTURAL DESIGN.	"This is what I looked like when dusk smote the light." Sound of volcanoes and dented tubas.
THE CITY IMPLODES IN A FREAKISH, ULTRAVIOLENT MAELSTROM. BUILDINGS INGEST FOLIAGE AND THEN COLLAPSE INTO A CENTRAL POINT IN THE FRAME. WHAT REMAINS IS A STARK WHITE FRAME WITH A STICKTHIN MAN AT	"This is what I looked like after dawn slaughtered the blackness." Sound of exultant, shining coronets.

ITS CENTER. HE WEARS A
BLACK SUIT AND BOWLER HAT.
CLEANSHAVEN. HANDSOME AND
REFINED. AND YET SOMETHING
ABOUT HIM STINKS OF THE
ORDINARY, THE PLAIN, THE
DEMORALIZED. THE UNNAMABLE.

SMILING, THE MAN TURNS AND
GOES WEST, KEEPING HIS EYES
ON THE AUDIENCE. CAMERA
FOLLOWS. HIS LIPS DO NOT
MOVE WHEN HE SPEAKS AND
LOOK LIKE THEY HAVE BEEN
GLUED ONTO HIS FACE.

Sir Edward Elgar's "Pomp
& Circumstance" March
No. 1 accompanies this
monologue, which is
uttered in a pleasant,
comfortable tessitura:
"Are you enormous? Has your
flesh accomplished galactic
proportions? Do you feel
powerless against your
corporeal bulk? Do you feel
that God has abandoned you,
and that an anxiety attack
lurks around every corner?
Eat a cookie and shed tons
and tons of leviathan gore.
That's what I did. That's
what I do."

THE MAN REMOVES A COOKIE
FROM AN INNER POCKET AND
PUTS IT TO HIS MOUTH. THE
LIPS WON'T OPEN. HE TOUCHES
THE COOKIE TO HIS MOUTH,

"Nabizko Higashis are
specially made to provide
you not only with crucial
fat-burning vitamins but the
mental willpower and moral

REPEATEDLY, EITHER IN AN
EFFORT TO PRY THE LIPS OPEN,
OR TO TEACH VIEWERS THAT
EATING IS ACHIEVED BY WAY OF
MULTIPLE ACTS OF BRINGING
FOOD TO ONE'S FACE.

A SERIES OF CODES FLICKER
INTO VIEW BENEATH THE MAN.

THE MAN STOPS WALKING AND
TURNS TO THE AUDIENCE.
SLOW-ZOOM. AFTER HE SPEAKS,
HE CHANGES BACK INTO A
CITY.

IT IS THE 2000TH TIME HE
HAS TURNED INTO KYOTO.

values to succeed. The more
cookies you eat, the more
weight you will lose. It's
that simple. They taste like
shit but the fuckers work.
That's a guarantee."

Sound of a choir hitting
a high note. "Just access
this sequence of codes. If
you access them within the
next seven minutes, we will
throw in a complimentary
hot dog and apple pie, both
with the same bulldozing
properties as Nabizko
Higashis."

"Nabizko Higashis. Isn't
it time for a change?"

二十一

the 3000th time I turned into Kyoto

DIAGNOSTIC PROSE

The sun had not yet risen on the mindscreen. It was a good mindscreen, and tasteful. The sea bled into the sky, but not to an estranging degree, and certainly not to a degree that the mindscreen offset the governing atmosphere and ambience of the restaurant.

His head resounded like a conch. One after another, waves broke upon the shore.

The. The.

On an angular dais...the skeleton of Steve McQueen. Not the real one. A *Bullitt* jacket hung from the shoulderbones. Tealights illuminated the skull sockets, the ribcage, the pelvis. Postmortem candelabra.

Otherwise the restaurant was conservatively decorated. Prosaic gaga aesthetics. A professional *Händler von Manierismus* on the farside of the restaurant tried to outshine the skeleton with intimidating tactics, but he was a freelance artist, uncontracted, and the sous-chefs chased him out of the establishment with great paring knives.

Deflation.

He couldn't keep his eyes off the skeleton. He often felt like Steve McQueen. In *Bullitt*.

Timecrash.

Everything changed. Everything but selfhood. Which was fluid, unfixed. Schizossified. A Body without Meaning (BwM).

—I think the timecrashes have stopped, he said. The woman narrowed heavily mascaraed eyes and took a deep breath, augmenting the line of her cleavage.

—Timecrash, she murmured. T-I-M-E-K-R-A-S-H-H-H.

—Indeed.

INFODUMP, OR, THY PILES

Only when he was nervous. He hated himself for it. An entirely superfluous word. Good for effekt only, and effekt, again and again, failed to sharpen the blades of Truth and Practicality.

—Indeed, he repeated.

—What's a timecrash?

INFODUMP, OR, THY PILES

There is nothing more modernist than the present moment. When one invades premodernist or postmodernist space, one arrives in Wonderland, and one's mind (d)evolves accordingly, ripping the mnemonic facilities to shreds and schlock. Thus timecrashes. Over the decades, or the centuries, or the months and weeks—however long they had been schizophrenizing the ballroom of reality— subjects' memories weathered like glass shards on a beach, surf and sand washing over them, smoothing out the sharp edges, the jagged spots, until all that remained were flat, featureless BwMs (Bodies without Mnemonics). This is one theory. Another posits that timecrashes have no effekt whatsoever on human memory. People merely forget themselves by nature. Additionally, few diagnostic minotaurs have accounted for the notion that the world may exist solely in the mind of one man, a superior being suffering from a nervous breakdown, just as Captain Ahab constituted every character in *Moby-Dick*. Stubbs, Starbuck, Queequeg, Tashtego, Daggoo, Flash, Pip, all subsidiary cannibals and savages and Nantucketeers, even the White Whale itself, and the *Pequod*, and storms, and the ocean, and the earth's equator, etc.—animate or inanimate, tangible or intangible, they are different illusory variations of the same monomaniac, born and bred from *corpus corporis exemplar*, products of a fragmented consciousness. "In the midst of the personified impersonal, a personality stands here," the old, grizzled fanatic says to himself. And then: "Is Ahab, Ahab?" No. Or rather, yes—but Ahab is also everybody else. And Ishmael is nothing but Ahab's mind's eye, or his dead soul, telling tall tales of the sea, and diagramming the vast, intricate bodies of leviathans, from some haunted house in the sky. And what goes for Ahab goes for Hamlet. And what goes for Hamlet goes for all of history's troubled/troublemaking protagonists.

Stampede of waiters.

—Where's our waiter? she asked. We've been sitting here for three minutes already. You haven't even told me your name. I know your name isn't Vlad Wallachia. That's a schizoid elective signature.

The. The.

He shuddered.

—I told you my name. You told me your name. What's your name? Well. Schizoverse dating doesn't work for everybody. Should we give up? You're better off. My insecurities transcend comprehension. But let's start over. I'll tell you my name and you tell me your name. Ok? My name is…Victor Gargantua.

—Victor Gargantua?

—Victor. Gargantua.

—That's a fake name.

—What's your fake name?

…

—Belinda. Belinda Carlisle. That's my *real* name. I'm not deranged.

—I'm not deranged.

—Then what's your real name.

…Plissken?

Plissken looked over his shoulder.

He looked over his shoulder.

He looked over his shoulder.

He couldn't stop looking over his shoulder. The skeleton of Steve McQueen unnerved him. It was looking at him. Communicating with him. Only him.

Waiter: roundeyed potbelly loud epaulette slit of mouth.

—May I refill your bulbs, he droned. It wasn't a question. He filled the empty bulbs with white table wine. It was the first time he had filled them. Somebody will be with you shortly. My name is _____.

Stampede of waiters.

One minute. Two minutes. Five minutes. Twenty minutes.

Waiter: slackeyed railthin unassuming epaulette slit of mouth.

—I'm starving to death, said Belinda. This restaurant is horrible, just horrible. I'm never coming back.

The waiter said:

—Let me tell you about our specials this evening. Rrrrrrsss. Karaaaaaaa. Pprrpffrrppfff.

—I'll have the _____, said Plissken. She'll have the _____.

—I don't want that.

—I'm a man, he growled, embarrassed by the outburst. Men take charge. You'll like it. Give it a chance.

—Let me refill your bulbs. The waiter filled the empty bulbs with white table wine. It was the first time he had filled them...

The décor of the restaurant featured rudiments from multiple eras. Only the keen eye could discern such a pastiche, and keen eyes rarely strayed from imaginary diegeses...Flatware from the Victorian period. Medieval goblets. Futique kambayashi chopsticks that could be telepathically manipulated. Metachronic artwork—deviant renderings of past and future celebrities in compromising positions; landscape paintings of Martian tundra. Walls coated in pop synaesthetics. Eighteenth century ceramic Spanish floortile. Yuppie tapestries. Glowglobes.

It occurred to the lay diner that s/he didn't know the name of the restaurant responsible for this plate of _____.

...the Chez Regardez?

Timecrashes may or may not have besieged the Chez Regardez. *Maintenant*. Like the spokes of a wheel, turning with such velocity that they looked static. These niggling atavisms. Petulance as the doppelgänger of charisma. Things changed. Reverse and fastforward. Things immobilized. Beat. Things went unnoticed.

INFODUMP, OR, THY PILES

...problematize timecrashes via different theories of time. There is the Newtonian theory, which dictates...overturned by Einstein's theory, which pronounces...early twentieth century. In recent years, quantum theorists have denounced the alleged "linearity" of time, favoring an arboreal model: infinite branches either grow from an originary trunk or, more probably, spread like a virus in the shape of a rhizome, sans origin. Others insist that time doesn't exist. Furthermore, as Barry Dainton writes, "relativistic cosmologists have argued that there may be a multiplicity of spacetimes (or 'baby universes') sprouting from the other end of black holes, and superstring theorists argue for the astonishing view that there are nine (or more) spatial dimensions" (*Time and Space* 4). Consequently any effort to define, categorize or grasp the meaning and/or vicissitudes of time spirals into reckless, pathological oblivion, like an exegesis without a thesis. The role of space complicates matters *bien plus*, space being the evil stepchild of time (and/or vice versa). Given this troubled dynamic, it is of course virtually impossible to grasp the nature of timecrashes. If we cannot come to a basic, tangible understanding of a "thing," how can we understand the perversions of the "thing"? And yet time is not a "thing." And yet it passes—we grow old...we grow old...our bodies wrinkle, wither. We die. They bury us in the sand.

...starting to get awkward. Belinda removed a tube of lipstick from her purse and smeared it onto her face. Plissken tried to conjure a viable topic.

—I wonder what aliens must think of human beings when they observe earth from their starships, mused Plissken. Particularly if they observe us having sex. Like, in a porno film. What if they mistook a porno for reality? We look so happy. There we are, naked and smiling. We make sounds that clearly indicate pleasurable sensations. We touch and lick and penetrate one another, and our facial expressions denote enjoyment. We like to twist our bodies into strange positions and wrap our limbs around one another. Some of us like to crap on one another. And so on. Is that what the aliens think of us? Or do they think, like, what the fuck are those assholes doing?

Belinda shifted uneasily in her seat.

—I'm not trying to make you uncomfortable. Honestly. It's a genuine concern. We're not a bunch of porno actors, after all. And we can assume that aliens exist. The universe is too fucking big. There has to be more intelligent life out there. Do you know how big the universe is? It's big. Like, beyond conception. Whether or not aliens are observing us is another question. Whether or not they are mistaking reality for a porno is still another question.

—This is...inappropriate. You're embarrassing me.

—Really? That wasn't my intent. Indeed. I mean, no. We don't have to talk about aliens. Or pornography. I can talk about other things. What should we talk about?

Waiter:...Dinner.

Delicious _____. And impeccably rendered. Plissken commanded the chopsticks to feed his mouth.

...He could feel the rice sliding down his esophagus. Moving too slowly. Clog...What next? If the exchange didn't pan out. Could be awkward. Could be mortal. Dead in the dining room. Floorkill.

GLP.

—Pardon me.

Belinda sipped a bulb of wine.

—I want to lose myself in your corpuscles, Plissken whispered. I want to take refuge within your tender buttons.

Belinda sipped a bulb of wine.

Women came and went, talking about hills like white elephants. The. He discovered it was Steve McQueen's real skeleton, not a simulacrum. A waiter leaned over and delivered the information into his ear like the last words of a man on death row. Unprompted. Validity as dread. The. The the. He stood and strode across the restaurant to inspect the skeleton and get to the bottom of the problem. The bottom nature of it. The the the the the thethetheheheeeeee...Reboot. Fear kept him at bay. He couldn't get close to it. He sat back down. Winded. Dotted with perspiration.

—Have you used Withaneyetocoitus.szv before? asked Belinda. She had concealed her cleavage in his absence, butterflying the fabric of her dress with a microcrystalline clothespin.

—It's hot in here. Jesus.

—I use Withaneyetocoitus.szv all the time. It's never worked for me. But I keep using it. I don't know why.

Plissken looked over his shoulder...

—Should they put candles on skeletons? Isn't that sacrilegious or something? I don't like it. What would Steve McQueen have said? I don't want anybody to put candles on my skeleton when I die. That's creepy.

He imagined that Belinda folded her elbows into her chest, and the clothespin came loose, opening her dress at the neck, and the dress slipped off of her shoulders and fell onto her hips, and she sat there before him, barebreasted and disruptive.

Dessert. They had not ordered it. Restaurant policy. Two white plates; brown nuclei.

Belinda pushed the dessert aside, climbed onto the table and crawled across it. Plissken's jaw dislocated. She kissed him. He didn't kiss back. Mouth open, frozen. She sucked on his lips and thrust her tongue into the speakhole, scouring the desiccated walls of the cavity, even nicking the epiglottis, and then flicking the epiglottis like a clitoris, anxious and forceful, as if trying to resuscitate a corpse. No response. She took him by the neck with one hand to brace herself while with her other hand she reached back and pulled her dress above her navel and yanked down her panties exposing the novum and she adroitly spun around the table onto his lap with a clang of utensils and a crash of dishware and faint splashes of wine spattered nearby patrons. She let go of his neck, grabbed his hair, jerked back his head—popping sound as their lips came apart—and unzipped his pants. Clockspring. She wounded herself on the slow knife. It was at this point he realized that Belinda had not attacked him but rather he had attacked her. She sat stiffly in her chair and he sat atop her, straddling her, rocking back and forth. A little circle had formed around them. Waiters and bus staff and the maître d'. They seemed pleased with the exhibition, delighted by its gravity and manner of broadcast, although something in their eyes, or their posture, indicated that they expected order to be restored within a reasonable span of time. Plissken quickened his pace. Then he heard it. The sound of transformation. Then he felt it. Welling up, creeping out. Bursting forth. His limbs cracked and knotted, contorting into impossible shapes. It was almost the 3000th time he turned into Kyoto. But before it happened he stopped himself. Dismounted the object. All was well. Not until later, outside, as he waited for a cab, reminiscing about the date, its highs and lows, how it might have turned out differently, wondering if Belinda Carlisle genuinely liked him and if he would see her again, for a second date, and a third and a fourth date, then marriage, kids, everything, but the thought of everything was too much, and suddenly, surprisingly, tragically, millions died, the city laid to waste, and Belinda flickered out, vanished into the grotto of history. Mnemonic vestiges. The. It was the 3000th time he turned into Kyoto. It was the only way this short chapter in his life could possibly end. And each chapter ended the same way. Unfinished. Usurped.

二十二

the 3001st time i turned into kyoto

CRITERION PROSE

They fought among the moocows and the curling flower spaces. This time they employed Factor Five Accelerators, purely for show, despite the absence of spectators, as the cyberware amped them up to the same speed. Both participants enjoyed the surreal euphoria that accompanied the augmentation, however, and afterwards, in the shower room, they idled like two pegheads coming down from near-fatal overdoses of Chew-Z.

"You almost beat me," remarked the doktor, nursing a sprained limb. "This has never happened before. What was that final maneuver?"

"*Subarashii tataku*. The Fabulous Swat. Let me show you again."

"No."

He executed the maneuver and the doktor lay on the floor like a doormat. "Goddamn it, Geoff," he rasped. "Keep that shit on the mat." He dryheaved.

"Geoff. Geoff?" He looked down at his arms, his legs, inspecting them as if they held the key to identity.

"Oh, pardon me." The doktor stood and adjusted his Adam's apple with a fingerblade. "I meant to say 'Geoff.' Enclosed in the whiskers of quotation marks, mind you. As with all names. What did Herr Amerika say? 'I was no longer I, I was "I," something in constant flux, a metamorph sucking on chunks of smooth rumperstiltskin.' This of course references a fundamental Baudrillardian theory, which itself references a fundamental Marxist theory, which accordingly reaches back to Kant, as everything reaches back to Kant, but there was life before Kant, of course. Case in point: names are always-already in quotes."

"Your name isn't in quotes."

"Some names are exceptions."

"What's your name?"

"You know my name. For sake of argument, however…Call me Fourmyle. Dr. Fourmyle."

"That's not your name."

"Must we do this every time we meet? Must you do this every day of your life? You're not an amnesiac. On occasion you exhibit symptoms of anterograde amnesia. But you simply don't have it."

"I have difficulty with names."

"Yes. I know. Hold that thought. Actually, negate that thought. Come with me."

"Geoff" followed Dr. Fourmyle into the shower. They did not touch one another. Pulsating scrubcrabs darted up and down their bodies and into their dark places. Tentacular hosepipes rinsed the suds. Sentient towelies relieved them, dried them. They dressed themselves.

"So," said Dr. Fourmyle as they took seats in his office. "How's it going?"

"Geoff" grinned wildly. "I met a girl."

"Hm. Tell me about her."

"There's not much to tell. She's a girl. A woman. Whatever. We went out to dinner at that place. That place in the city."

"Hm. Where did you meet her?"

"The schizoverse. Withaneyetocoitus.szv."

"Ah yes."

"I'm not ashamed."

"Nor should you be. How did it go then? The date."

"I don't know. Fine, I guess. Typical. A date's a date. Steve McQueen's skeleton was in the corner."

"Did you meet her in the schizoverse or the real world?"

"We met in the schizoverse. We went out in the real world. Kind of."

"Kind of."

"Yeah. Anyway, what does it matter? I met a girl, is all. That's what matters."

"I see. Will you date her a second time?"

"No."

"Why not?"

"Geoff" paused. "I dispatched her."

Dr. Fourmyle leaned into his swivelchair. He put his arms behind his head and twisted back and forth on his heels. "I don't exercise as much as I used to," he remarked. "It's not that I don't have time either. I simply choose not to exercise as much as I used to."

"Geoff" couldn't tell if he was trying to redirect the conversation. He didn't care. "I don't know what's wrong with me. I transformed against my will. I thought I had control of myself. But I'm out of control."

The doktor leaned forward. "You've just described the human condition. The gaining of control, the loss of control, the regaining of control. Mankind."

"That's not helpful. That's not helpful, ok? I'm telling you it's getting bad." "Geoff" rubbed his eyes.

"The," said the doktor.

"The?"

"The."

"The what?"

"Whatever you want. You finish."

"Geoff" sighed through his teeth. He fell silent. Then: "Sometimes I can't tell if I'm living in a dream, a novel, a film, a TV show, a talk show, a soda commercial, a music video, a figment of **Travis Manderbean**'s imagination, the real world, or some perverse combination of these media."

"Yes. You have expressed this idea the last 400 or so times we sparred, albeit the figure in whose mind you claim to exist as a figment always changes. Last time it was Sophocles. The time before last it was Napoleon. Once it was Jason Robards. Who is **Travis Manderbean?**"

"I don't know. A disc jockey, I think."

"What is a disc jockey?"

"Forget it."

"All right. Perhaps if we tried a little hypnosis. Let's do that." Dr. Fourmyle opened a drawer and removed a large gold medallion on a string.

"Put that away. Hypnosis doesn't work on me. You know that."

"If we keep at it, it might. Someday."

"It won't. Ever."

"You don't know that. People change. One day they are incapable of one thing. The next day they can do anything."

"People don't change. They think they do, but they don't."

Dr. Fourmyle dropped the medallion in the drawer. "All right. Let's return to your date. Let's talk about this woman you dispatched. No. Let's broaden our scope. Let's talk about why you've never been married. You're not a young man."

"How do you know I've never been married? Maybe I have. Maybe I'm married now. With kids."

"You're not married. You don't have children." The doktor tapped a finger against his skull and pointed at his groin.

"Geoff" shrugged. "Whatever. I don't know. A wife? Kids? I can't even take care of myself…I'm a serial killer."

"Hm."

"Fuck you."

"According to Herr Freud, males strive for autonomy with their mother. Failure to obtain autonomy culminates in rage. Hence serial killing. Hence we must address the following issue: Mother."

"Fuck you."

"Did she neglect you? Or did she pay too much attention to you? There are only two options."

Something loud passed by outside a window. A helicopter. Perhaps a small plane that had flown too close to the building.

The roar of machinery came and went.

"Mother contracted Alzheimer's disease when I was three years old," said "Geoff." "By the time I turned four, she had forgotten who I was. It was very hard for me. Then, when I was six, Mother got better—the Alzheimer's went away. It came back again when I was eleven, though. Then it went away, and then it came back, and then it went away, and then it came back. Fuck me. She kept forgetting and remembering me. I was confused. Then she died."

"Neglect, then. And your father?"

"He died. Everybody's dead. I killed them all."

"Hm."

"Fuck you."

"I'm going to prescribe you a dose of _____. Immediately. It will help."
Dr. Fourmyle dialed the pharmacy. Seconds later, a thin metal canister emerged
from a chute in the wall and rolled across his desk. He secured the canister,
opened it, and dumped out a pill bottle. He gave it to "Geoff," who opened the
pill bottle and swallowed the contents. Dr. Fourmyle poured a small glass of
water and gave it to "Geoff." He drank it.

They waited.

"That helped," said "Geoff."

"I told you it would."

"What was that?"

"*Druuugs.*"

"Geoff" reclined on the chaise. He turned onto his side and curled up his
legs. "I don't know how people negotiate timecrashes and zoneshifts. With
or without medication. Time is displaced in the mind at any given moment.
Mnemonically, I mean. On the mindscreen, we're always reaching back into
the swill of memory and imagining potential futures. What happens when we
actually, physically move through time? Psyche and the Body are terminally
fused. Schized. We all go crazy."

"If everybody is crazy, there is no crazy. There is only normal."

"Geoff" turned onto his other side. "The world becomes more science
fictionalized every day. The present moment has teeth; it devours endless
potential futures. The same goes for the past. We experience endless waves of
medievalization. And more. I once found myself wandering across the vastness
of Pangea like Clint Eastwood in a Spaghetti western, fighting off dinosaurs,
gunslingers and technocapitalists in equal measure. Space elevators loomed
overhead. I have seen the moon explode and grow back like a cyst on the skin
of the sky. I have seen the human pipe bomb at its most explosive—body parts
toppled into the abyss spurting gore from thrashing fleshtubes. I have stood on
the lip of a black hole and dared the animal to suck me into oblivion. I shared
a tepid pint of beer with Charles Dickens in a pub in Soho. He told me he was

Jack the Ripper. Windmills attacked me like Nephilim and I pulverized their menacing projections with a bangsword. I was a teenage werewolf. I directed films and orchestras and soldiers into battle. Then I invented celluloid and the French horn and the art of war. Bronx cheers followed me like bloodhounds desperate for their master's affection. Extraterrestrial homunculi abducted and probed me. I killed them. Pharaohs penetrated me. I killed them. Troglodytes drew pictures of me on cave walls. I tolerated them. I robbed a bank with my index finger and thumb. I incited a stellar evolution. I fucked everyone and everything, everywhere, in the ass. I galvanized my soul, proving its immunity to existence. There is no end to my fearsome ubiquity. The future, the past. They constantly implode into the present, into a central point...I am that central point. I am the present. I am..."

As "Geoff" continued, Dr. Fourmyle called in another prescription...

GLP.

"And will you dispatch me at the end of this session?" inquired the doktor after a long, satisfying pause. "Will you transform into the monster and render me your victim yet again? One shot and that's the end of the vulture. *Ein Schuß und der Geier ist erledigt.*"

"I don't know what will happen," said "Geoff." "I don't feel well. I know that."

"Every day is a new day. Tomorrow you may feel better."

"Geoff" closed his fingers into a fist and studied the vascularity of his forearm. A rhizome of veins inflated and came to life. He flexed and reflexed his forearm until it seemed as if the veins might burst.

It was the 3001st time he turned into Kyoto.

十三

the 4000th time i turned into kyoto
CRITERION PROSE

"And so it begins," thunders a voice from beyond the Curve.

Cameras equipped with intervelometer devices produce timelapse effekts. The shutter fires at exacting intervals and characters appear to move in uncanny bursts of flashtime...

A spaceman floats beyond the ninth circle of the Martian atmosphere. He wears a bloodred spacesuit, tight against the skin, and a disproportionate bubble helmet. A seminal strand of liquid oxygen leaks from a crack in his jetpack.

Across the vacuous ocean, we hear the faint sound of MTV's first promotional segment, guitars blasting as spacemen erect an animated Technicolor flag on the surface of the ghostwhite moon.

Stark pause.

The spaceman erupts into a city. Tendrils of architecture infect the void... Optic pandemonium. Flashing strobes. Volcanic rumble as the city expands, unfolds, clanks and locks into place...

Pan out 200,000 miles.

Cast in silhouette, the city floats across the red eye of Mars like an amorphous pupil. No noise. No music.

The city is empty. Always empty...

A spaceman in a jetpack appears as if from a covert wormhole. He isn't wearing a spacesuit. He looks like Johnny Cash—black hair, black leather jacket, black cowboy shirt, black jeans, black boots. Instead of a guitar he carries a tremendous, fiery Buster sword.

His name is Cyrano Nightranger.

He floats across the void towards the city.

Within minutes, they engage in battle. Nightranger and the city trade blow after blow against crescendos of excited, synthesized trumpets. Nightranger is wounded, rallies. The city is wounded, rallies. Back and forth they hack at one another, losing flesh and blood and wood and oil, until Nightranger finally succumbs to the Inevitable and the void receives his severed limbs and neon entrails...

"Crap!" rasped Daryl. Weakly, he hammered the joystick against a console.

Freddy smiled a rotten smile. "I win again," he said. "You can't beat me."

Daryl exercised his fingers. They were yellow and bony and liverspotted with brittle, flaking nails. They ached so much more when he and Freddy weren't playing the game. He said, "Nightranger did it in real life. I can do it here."

Freddy's laugh flattened into a meek cough. "That's a legend," he wheezed. "Nightranger never killed the city. This is, like, the 4000th time I've beat you. You're not gonna beat me. It can't happen."

"There's always a loophole."

The hovel in which they had taken refuge was on the verge of collapse. The slightest wind produced long, loud creaks, and whenever an escape shuttle flew overhead, the walls came apart a little more, flooding the hideout with dust and asbestos. Daryl and Freddy were both thoroughly emaciated, the knobs of their spines forming an obscene curve beneath tattered, bloodstained shirts. They dryheaved regularly, as if garroted, abdominal muscles convulsing like strangled tongues. Freddy had an open sore on his neck that leaked pus and blood with slow resolution. The hovel might have been a kitchen once, cluttered with the twisted, blackened remnants of appliances from ceiling to floor. The only thing that worked was the gaming system...

INFODUMP, OR, THY PILES

...which the boys protected with their lives, like a mother protects her young. On the cusp of global apocalypse, they had decided not to leave earth. Their parents were dead. Their siblings and friends were dead. They were too far in the outrézone to get out anyway.

Everything had been trodden and razed, as if by some galactic steamroller. Vestiges of life persisted in the aftermath. There were three kinds: predators, prey, and

men with resources. The latter camp had fled; now they
sailed across space and time towards the Unknown. That
left the others. The meateaters. The meat.

The boys had hotwired an Atari 5200 to a Nintendo
Vorga. They had been playing **The Kyoto Man** for days.
How many days they didn't know, but they knew they
had not slept since the last holocaust. Nor had they eaten.
Only a few dogpoets lingered in the outrézone. Either the
dogpoets would find and dispatch Freddy and Daryl, or
they would die playing a video game that they prized more
than life itself.

Either way, the boys would die like men.

"Again," said Daryl, caressing the joystick. He dryheaved and flushed
purple.

Grimly, Freddy turned to the mindscreen, a bubble of bloody pus escaping
the lesion in his neck. "And so it begins…"

二十四
the 5000th time I turned into Kyoto
ASTOUNDING STORY

Dr. Josef Mengele was doing something bad. Voiceman **Travis Manderbean** stood nearby and narrated the event.

"He's really gone too far this time, folks," said **Manderbean**. He wore a cheap yellow blazer and held a 1950s rockabilly microphone to his lips. "How he flouts convention. How he cracks open the bad eggs. I daresay no man has bore witness to such a shocking carnival of subjugation. Truly this hatemonger is the embodiment of unchecked human misery. My name is **Travis Manderbean**."

Daylight fell on the slave plantation. There was a cottonfield to the left, and a cornfield to the right, and bright green grass beneath their feet, and behind them rose the towering white pillars of the landowner's mansion. Nobody remembered how or when they had arrived at the plantation. They might have been there all along.

Dr. Mengele had adopted the role of slavemaster. His hair was disheveled and cropped in a considered, négligé style with a long ear-to-ear curl that fell over the top of the head. A cocked-brimmed hat lay on the grass at his feet. He had on white breeches, a red muslin neckerchief, and a brown double-breasted riding coat with a high collar and broad lapels. Striped silk stockings terminated in buckled black shoes. In one hand he held a flexible, razorsharp sword, in the other a leather bullwhip, weapons he only put aside for seconds at a time so that he could light fresh cigarettes. Marlboros.

Dr. Mengele spoke the twangy, elastic American English of a third generation Southerner. The objects of his aggression, contrary to the Laws of Assumption, were not African slaves, but giant blobs of tissue, sallow and veined and amorphous, like larvae. Blurred eyeholes and contorted mouths materialized in the head region and emitted a dense fog that poured across the lawn. The creatures twitched fiercely when they were whipped, and when they were stabbed, they leaked a diseased, mustard-colored soot. They refused to expire. Dr. Mengele had even lopped one in half, with no small effort, as if chopping a fallen tree, cartoon entrails and gristle spattering his face and erupting into the sky, but the halves became their own entities, prompting the doktor to discipline and punish them with more resolve.

"They scream like grasshoppers," narrated **Manderbean**, a crooked smile swinging from his chin like an anchor. "When one hears a grasshopper scream, one doesn't soon forget it. I repeat: they scream like grasshoppers. And they bleed like leviathans. Once I stripped a whale of its blubber from nose to tail and what I'm witnessing here, ladies and gentlemen, confirms that I was not the victim of mere incantatory desire. Allow me the hairy arm of elaboration. I slayed the whale with a tomahawk. The daemon bore its monstrous head, rising open-mouthed from the hoary depths as if to swallow the firmament, and I leapt from the mainmast, fell the length of the Terminal Tower, and buried the hatchet in its blowhole. There was a great struggle during which the goliath and I wrestled like titans, turning and turning in the widening gyre. I, **Travis Manderbean**, won the battle. In the aftermath, I tore open the carcass and bathed in spermaceti and blubber—precisely in the fashion of our antagonist, now, here, before me, and before the eyes of the entire ruined world. One needs no cameras to perform on the stage of life. But it appears the mad doktor grows weary. Fatigue is a dirty slut. See how his breathing becomes more erratic. See how his knees threaten to buckle. Soon he will collapse. If only the man had access to a reliable energy drink. But this is history, and like solar whores, we must filch our energy from the sun."

An out-of-control stagecoach clattered by on unstable wheels. Nobody manned the helm and the Clydesdales had red eyes. The stagecoach was pursued by a group of Spaniards riding vehicles that resembled overturned windmills. Flames roared from exhaust pipes.

Travis Manderbean took a stiff breath. "But what's this?"

She stepped from the porch of the mansion and moved towards them. **Manderbean** didn't question her dubious appearance; he had given up on Time long ago—not to mention Presence, Absence, and Acceptable Flows of Reality. Now he went to great lengths to make light of her, shifting his attention from Dr. Mengele to this being who, thus spake that **Zarathustra**, "might have once appeared on the book cover of a bodice-ripping romance or a pulp science fiction novel in which masculine bonecrushers defeat terrible adversaries so as to receive the prize of scantily clad ladies bearing preternaturally supersized breasts. I doubletake her glands even as I speak. Somebody has soaped them up with a wet sponge. They sway back and forth like bedtime stories as she moves closer, dripping suds. The nipples are hard and the cleavage is deep. Such elegant red lipstick—prior to this experience I didn't know that shade of red existed. Without bias, I tell you the substance reposes on her lips like fresh aftershock. This is **Travis Manderbean**. Note the slit that runs up her skirt and exposes a limber white thigh. The skirt is diaphanous—I observe nimble panties that conceal the shadow of a frozen scream. What wide buttocks. What wild ecstasy. But above all we must concern ourselves with the glands. The glands are the things. Life-sucking, life-giving. No man would not want to hold and possess them. Here they come, folks. Brace yourselves for eternity."

Dr. Mengele's agitation spiked as **Manderbean** continued to ignore his actions and devote his narrational vitality to the "Damsel without a Dulcimer," as he began to call her. To complicate matters, the plantation was under attack. A battalion of corny-looking, saucer-shaped UFOs had swooped down from the troposphere. They fired precise raybeams at the mansion, blowing holes in its smooth beige siding. **Manderbean** didn't waste time documenting the absurdity. "If they are not extra-terrestrials," he observed, "whence did they come? No matter. I pledge to you that these otherworldly hooligans are mere figments of my collective unconscious, just as everything and everyone are figments of my collective unconscious. The truth hurts. Lies are the price of life."

Suddenly the woman stood before **Manderbean** like an apparition. They gazed into one another's eyes, the hot sun penetrating their skin. "We are gazing into one another's eyes," **Manderbean** said, echoing Eternity, "with the hot sun penetrating our skin. Perhaps the gaze will culminate in a kiss?" He tossed aside the microphone.

They kissed. Violently. **Manderbean** grabbed the woman by the elbows and shook her.

…the blobs withered.

Infuriated, Dr. Mengele lashed at the blobs with the whip, throwing all of his strength into the chore. **Manderbean** didn't break the kiss; he caught the end of the whip just as it snapped, then flicked his wrist and sent a ripple in the opposite direction that kicked the butt of the handle into the underside of

Mengele's chin, and the Nazi's feet came out from under him. He fell to the ground, struck his head on a rock in the grass, and lost consciousness.

He awoke. Everything was gone. Literally. The landscape. The props. The earth. He stood there...No, he didn't stand...He hung there...No, he didn't hang...He simply _____ there, which is to say, nowhere, no place. Utopia.

The void was colorless. It looked like this:

Dr. Mengele blinked.

Travis Manderbean pinched the bridge of his nose and removed the smiling faceplate.

It was him.

"You," said Dr. Mengele.

"Don't be afraid," he assured him. "My existence is in perfect harmony with the laws of science." He gripped Dr. Mengele's neck and gently strangled him. The doktor struggled to no avail.

"This is the last time," he whispered.

Dr. Mengele wheezed, "Why're ya doin' this to me?"

"You are an antagonist. I am a protagonist. I have killed you on thousands of occasions. This is the last time."

"P-poisoner of all nations...Why me?"

"I have known and killed infinite supervillains, on infinite occasions, in infinite timeframes, spatialities and metaphysical stadiums. You are not special. You are stardust and I am the sun. I don't expect you to understand. I don't expect anything from anybody. I have moved beyond the chariot of time, the hammer of reality. This is my universe. Your eyes can't hit what your hands can't see."

"The Jews," said Mengele.

He snapped the doktor's neck. The corpse burst into thin gray flakes and caved into an air pocket...

"...I stood beside the bed and he was sitting up between the sheets, clad in his underwear, with a great portfolio in his hands...Beauty and the Beast... Loneliness...Old Grocery Horse...Brook'n Bridge..."

Then, hunched over a desk, I extracted an implant from the small of my neck. Using duct tape, industrial twine, and ionized copper flanges, I had arranged a series of three rearview mirrors in such a way that I could monitor the operation. The implant looked and felt like a segment of barbwire. It had been wrapped around the cerebellum and the medulla, squeezing the units together. My vision flickered as valuable brain tissue frayed and shredded. A warm fluid issued from the wound and trickled down the skin of my back. There was a dull sonic hum. I cleaned the implant with a toothbrush and placed it on the desktop. It looked like seaweed. It glowed. I picked up the implant and turned it over in my hands, searching for distinctive marks or insignia. I couldn't find any. I used a magnifying glass, an electron microscope. Nothing. At last I examined the implant with a soulfinder capable of detecting spiritual bodies in inanimate objects. I found a spirit—a blob of tissue, sallow and veined and amorphous. Something had been tattooed onto its hide. This:

I deduced the cipher's meaning and purpose, then second-guessed my conclusions. I rethought the matter and overturned conflicting results that I summarily flouted and overturned again. Subtitles flared onto the mindscreen. I couldn't remember where I had read them. I spoke them aloud:

"The mountain...is a symbol."

I decided that 山 was some kind of superhero icon. The decision nearly mirrored my initial hermeneutic, but not without significant *différence*, rendering it unique and singular, the very antithesis of a reflection, vague or otherwise. I stood and went to the bathroom to take my medication and dress the wound, hoping I would remain in the present, at least until I had stopped the bleeding. It felt as if my brain had leaked out. Memories escaped me like exhaust fumes. Must regain control. I breathed deeply, evenly, and articulated my mantra. Ohhm. Zhhh. Avoid history at all costs. Sssss. Deflect the future via orchestral maneuvers in the dark. Haaaaaa. Float like a bee, sting like a butterfly...

二十五
the boooth time i turned into kyoto
MOVIE RATING

THE FOLLOWING **DIEGESIS** HAS BEEN APPROVED FOR

ALL AUDIENCES

BY THE STICK FIGURE ASSOCIATION OF AMERIKA

THE DIEGESIS ADVERTISED HAS BEEN RATED

METROMORPHIC

Some Material My Be Inappropriate for Robosapiens, Clockwork Men & Superior Persons

FOR HIGHFALUTIN LANGUAGE, SEXUAL INFLECTION, PHALLIC HYSTERIA IN THE RAW,
ARCHITECTURES OF DREAD, OLD SCHOOL ULTRAVIOLENCE & SOME CHAINSMOKING

二十六
the 7000th time I turned into Kyoto
SOUND & FURY DISABLED REMIX

one minute she was standing there the next he was yelling & pulling at her dress

strangebrew from man into monster
I accidentally ingest a photograph & the photograph (en)frames me like a polaroid
at first I think its athletes foot but its metromorphia
the neon stalks exacerbate my condition
ira überstein rules the world
nobody can stop him
power emanates most effektively from indefatigable orifices & I have only seen
überstein once in real life
he recurs in my antidreams & greases the engine of the nightmare of reality
now the chorus:

jigsaw city & the rot of scag media
kisses the future, stings like pangea
gonna git high, gonna dance all nite
gonna hack off the sky with my razorsharp kite

her face looked at the sky it was low so low that all smells & sounds of night seemed to have been crowded down like under a slack tent

in "the metropolis & mental life" georg simmel inscribes: "the deepest problems of modern life derive from the claim of the individual to preserve the autonomy & individuality of his existence in the face of overwhelming social forces, of historical heritage, of external culture, & of the technique of life." simmel takes a drag from a cigarette. "the psychological basis of the metropolitan type of individuality consists in the intensification of nervous stimulation which results from the swift & uninterrupted change of outer and inner stimuli. man is a differentiating creature. his mind is stimulated by the difference between a momentary impression & the one which preceded it. lasting impressions, impressions which differ only slightly from one another, impressions which take a regular & habitual course & show regular & habitual contrasts—all these use up, so to speak, less consciousness than does the rapid crowding of changing images, the sharp discontinuity in the grasp of a single glance, & the unexpectedness of onrushing impressions." another drag. "these are the psychological conditions which the metropolis creates."

the city in question is a grannysknot of broken circuits.

the city in fritz langs film <u>metropolis</u> is made of cardboard. the aerial shots are cartoons.

the city in <u>blade runner</u> is a miniaturized reproduction of an extrapolated los angeles (trans. lost angles).

the city in every noir film is the same city. dark & sharp. thin smirks of light.

the city of liverpool is an ode to the beatles to the titanic to workingclass despair. a stoic cathedral rises from its highest summit. graveyard in the backyard.

winter. devotchkas in colorful lingerie & makeup stroll up & down the icy sidewalks searching for viable discotheques & fish & chip shops. I can see them from the tall window.

totem poles of department stores & restaurants & gentlemen's clubs. the whiteness of the whale. vancouver.

Im finagling her asterisk. Im in the crowsnest.

the flying island-city of laputa hovers over the ground-city of lagado. everyone can hear the flappers whipping the laputians & preserving mnemonic order.

hong kong is an island city of the future beneath which swim the dragondolas of history. I remember the commute from kowloon. mirrored buildings. blue sky. I smelled flowers & fish.

see meditation xvii. & yet.

chorus

she looked at me then everything emptied out of her eyes & they looked like the eyes in statues blank & unseeing & serene

the sky the surf the wind in my hair
infinite & spontaneous roots of evil complement sudden eruptions of ultraviolence e.g. fireballs explode from quiet flesh e.g. tentacles explode from quiet flesh e.g. imperial palaces explode from quiet flesh
from space earth looks like a decayed apple lodged between the segments of a scorched vermin oppressed by a bearded patriarch hence infinite letters to the father
the lobsters stare out of the aquarium in polite agony

chorus

her blood surged steadily beating & beating against my hand

tcz
we all prefer chew-z to can-d
a noblemans private xanadu can be gleaned via the katsura detached palace with its cherry blossoms & tastefully situated rocks & long ago the kinkakuji temple of the golden pavilion served as a retirement villa for aged ninjas & etched into the stone torii gates of the yasaka-jinja yasaka shrine are rumors of utopia & maruyama park & kurodani temple a giant granite nephilim in the parking lot smiling like a buddha over a sea of toyotas mazdas hondas nissans subarus isuzus mitsubishis mad dash of nordic tourists my father took a picture of me at the foot of the nephilim I wore a black blazer & blue jeans with arms akimbo & I searched all day for a sake grenade I wasnt sure what kind I wanted but nothing felt right & then I found what I was looking for in a shop that had been made to look like a cave the unassuming porcelain grenade accompanied by two miniscule handmade cups & in the wake of my purchase the vendor urged me

never to drink my sake cold

you may think Im disabled but I promise I will plagiarize again bootlegging the
lesser gods

play it again "sam"

the sky the surf the wind in my hair

Im a secret agent & Im a superzero & I tell everyone my name

this is he 7000th time Ive turned into Kyoto

but in the end it doesnt ratiocinate

apathy spills into the gulag

no one eats breakfast on mercurial doomsday

because no one is home

writ de lunatico

Im a raging *daikaiju* & Im a *fin de mundo tetsuo* & I will turn this fucking world
to rust & I will roost upon the wasteland like a beakless chauntecleer despite the
eternal rorschachs of dystrophy

chorus

chorus

chorus

二十七

the 3000th time I turned into kyoto

TELESCRIPT

SEASON 5, EPISODE 120: TITLE UNKNOWN

FADE IN.

SCENE [X]

<u>EXT.OXFORD UNIVERSITY</u> - DAY

<u>OSCAR WILDE</u> (20s) SAUNTERS ACROSS THE FINELY TRIMMED
CAMPUS OF OXFORD UNIVERSITY TOTING A LOBSTER ON A
LEASH. HE WEARS A PINK CRAVAT, FRILLED SHIRT, AND
PINSTRIPED TROUSERS TUCKED INTO KNEE-HIGH EQUESTRIAN
BOOTS. HE HOLDS HIS CHIN HIGH, KICKING UP HIS HEELS
AND GESTICULATING WITH HIS FREE ARM AS IF CONDUCTING
AN ORCHESTRA OF INCORRIGIBLE AMATEURS. THE LOBSTER
SEEMS TO HOLD ITS HEAD UP, TOO, LEGS CLACKING AGAINST
THE COBBLESTONE WALKWAY.

EVENTUALLY, INEVITABLY, <u>A GROUP OF STUDENTS BEAT UP</u>
<u>WILDE AND STOMP ON THE LOBSTER</u>. THE CRUSTACEAN'S
WHITE VISCERA EXPLODES FROM ITS CRACKED SHELL. WILDE
LIMPS BACK TO HIS DORM ROOM, DRAGGING THE DEAD PET
BEHIND HIM...

<u>STOP</u>. THE WRITERS REALIZE THAT THIS NARRATIVE WON'T
SUFFICE FOR AN EPISODE OF *THE TWILIGHT ZONE*. SERLING
IS MAD. <u>BACKUP</u>. <u>REWRITE</u>.

SCENE [X] – TAKE 2

INT.COURTROOM – DAY

THE COURTROOM IS VAST AND GRAY. WE CAN'T SEE THE CEILING.
A STERN CHANCELLOR (50s) SITS BEHIND A FARCICALLY
TALL ALTAR. A MALE SECRETARY (40s) SITS AT THE HEAD
OF A FARCICALLY LONG TABLE. OBSCURE MEN AND WOMEN IN
PLAINCLOTHES FILL OUT THE RANKS. TWO THIN, TOWERING DOORS
EASE OPEN AND THE FRAIL SHADOW OF AN OBSOLETE MAN (50s)
POURS ACROSS THE FLOOR. HE WALKS FORWARD TO BE JUDGED.
AN ELDERLY GATEKEEPER (90s) WEARING AN EXECUTIONER'S
MASK BARS HIS WAY AND TAKES HIM BY THE ELBOW.

                    GATEKEEPER
                     (FIRMLY)
          No admittance.

                    OBSOLETE MAN
                   (DISHEARTENED)
          Will I be allowed in later?

                    GATEKEEPER
                    (SHRUGGING)
          It is possible. But I am not
          particular.

THE CHANCELLOR SLAMS A GAVEL INTO THE ALTAR, DEMANDING
ORDER IN THE COURT.

                    OBSOLETE MAN
              (SQUINTING AT THE CHANCELLOR)

I know you. And I want nothing to
say to you.

                    CHANCELLOR
                (WILDLY DICTATORIAL)
Control that obsolete man, sir, or
I shall make you into a clerk!

                    GATEKEEPER
                (PEJORATIVELY)
I would prefer not to take a
clerkship.

THE OBSOLETE MAN BECOMES ANXIOUS. <u>HE BEGINS TO TREMBLE</u>
WITH EQUAL AMOUNTS OF RAGE AND PANIC.

                    OBSOLETE MAN
I want to come in. I demand a
sentence. I demand admittance to
the Law. I have passed through
the gate. Now it's your turn.

                    CHANCELLOR
                (IN A BOOMING VOICE)
This gate was made only for you!
And now I am going to shut it!

                    OBSOLETE MAN
But now, when the ethical is
thus teleologically suspended,
how does the single individual
in whom it is suspended exist?

PLAINCLOTHES WOMAN
(FROM OFFSCREEN)
Ah Bartleby! Ah shiteaters!

<u>STOP</u>. THIS IS ESSENTIALLY THE SAME PLOT AS THE BEGINNING
OF EPISODE 29, SEASON 2, "THE OBSOLETE MAN," WITH MINOR
DIFFERENCES, E.G., THE DIALOGUE HAS BEEN RECKLESSLY
PLAGIARIZED FROM MELVILLE'S "BARTLEBY THE SCRIVENER,"
KIERKEGAARD'S *FEAR & TREMBLING*, AND A DUMB TRANSLATION
OF KAFKA'S PARABLE "BEFORE THE LAW." SERLING IS MAD.
HE INSISTS THAT EVERY EPISODE BE AUTHENTIC AND UNIQUE;
ONLY A SMALL MARGIN OF EXTRAPOLATION IS PERMISSABLE.
AND YOU CAN'T SWEAR ON TV. HE BADMOUTHS THE WRITERS,
THEN ATTACKS THEM WITH AIRHAMMERS... <u>BACKUP</u>. <u>REWRITE</u>.

SCENE [X] - TAKE 3

<u>INT.TWILIGHT ZONE SET</u> - DAY

<u>ROD SERLING</u> (40s), WEARING A WOOL SHARKSKIN SUIT,
CIGARETTE IN ONE HAND, CUP OF COFFEE IN THE OTHER,
DELIVERS AN OPENING MONOLOGUE IN "BURNING CHROME"
BLACK-AND-WHITE. HALFWAY THROUGH THE MONOLOGUE HE
FORGETS WHO HE IS AND WHAT HE'S SAYING. HE ASKS SOMEBODY
TO REFRESH HIS MEMORY AND THE <u>AUTOCUE OPERATOR</u> (20s)
THREATENS TO CALL THE POLICE IF HE DOESN'T GET OFF
THE SET SO THAT THEY CAN SHOOT THE GODDAMNED EPISODE.
SERLING FIRES HIM. THE AUTOCUE OPERATOR CALLS THE
POLICE. <u>TWO POLICEMAN</u> (20s) COME AND ARREST SERLING.
THE CHARGE: HE IS A NAZI AND AN EVIL VENTRILOQUIST
DOLL. HE RESISTS ARREST AND <u>THE POLICEMEN PIN HIM</u>
<u>DOWN AND THROTTLE HIM WITH BILLYCLUBS</u>; HIS WOUNDS

PULSE AND EXPLODE LIKE SQUIBS. THE WRITERS NOD IN
SATISFACTION. DURING THE MELEE SERLING'S FACEPLATE
COMES LOOSE AND FALLS OFF, REVEALING AN INTRICATE
MICROWAVE CIRCUIT CARD. HE IS NOT A NAZI DEVIL-
DOLL AFTER ALL BUT MASKATRON, SWORN ENEMY OF THE
SIX MILLION DOLLAR MAN. CURIOUSLY, MASKATRON DID NOT
APPEAR ON THE CRITICALLY ACCLAIMED 1970s TELEVISION
SHOW. MANUFACTURED BY THE KENNER TOY COMPANY, HE
WAS AN ACTION FIGURE BASED UPON THE CHARACTER MAJOR
FREDERICK SLOAN IN THE EPISODE "DAY OF THE ROBOT" IN
WHICH A MAN IS REPLACED BY AN ANDROID DOPPELGÄNGER
FOR "CIRCUITOUS" PURPOSES.

SERLING LEAPS TO HIS FEET, CLOTHESLINES BOTH POLICEMEN
WITH ONE ARM AND RUNS OUTSIDE.

EXT.YOKNAPATAWPHA - DAY

AN AIRPLANE FLIES OVERHEAD. SERLING JUMPS INTO THE
SKY AND LANDS ON A WING. THE SUN MELTS OFF HIS FACE.
HE RIPS APART HIS CLOTHES. HE IS AN ALIEN. HIS
TEETH ARE SHARP, HIS COUNTENANCE HIDEOUS. HE HAS
NO GENITALS AND HIS SPINE SQUIRMS BENEATH THE SKIN
LIKE A MUTANT CENTIPEDE. HE GLARES INTO THE WINDOWS,
ANTAGONIZING THE PASSENGERS... THE AIRPLANE CRASHES
INTO A MOUNTAIN, BUT SERLING MANAGES TO LEAP ONTO A
TREETROP BEFORE THE FLAMES ENGULF...

STOP.

ROD SERLING
(FROWNING)

Actually that's not bad.

BUT SOMETHING TELLS HIM HE HAS BEEN (RE)MADE INTO THE
BUTT OF A JOKE...BACKUP...

SCENE [X] - TAKE 4

THIS FOURTH REWRITE CENTERS ON THE KYOTO MAN AND EXPLAINS
HIS PREDICAMENT. THE SCENE BEGINS WITH THE GRUESOME MURDER
OF ROD SERLING FOLLOWED BY A CONSIDERABLE MEASURE OF
EXPOSITION DURING WHICH THE GLOBAL EFFEKTS OF THE KYOTO
MAN'S RELENTLESS EXISTENCE ARE CLARIFIED, DENIGRATED AND
LAMENTED. WE ALSO DISCOVER THAT THE UNIVERSE ENTERTAINS
NO LIFE OTHER THAN HUMAN LIFE, I.E., "THE EARTH IS THE
ONLY BIOLOGICALLY FERTILE BALL OF OIL AND EVERYTHING
ELSE IS BLACK HOLES, FIRE, AND DEAD WEIGHT."

AT SERLING'S FUNERAL, THE KYOTO MAN GIVES THE EULOGY. HE
GOES ON AND ON ABOUT SERLING'S PRIVATE LIFE, CHRONICALLY
REPEATING THE WORD "MASCULINITY." FOR INSTANCE:

THE KYOTO MAN
Nobody could make a martini like
Rod. I suspect this had something
to do with a deep understanding
of masculinity.

THE KYOTO MAN
Mark my words: the phrase "raw masculinity" will come to be associated
exclusively with the life and times
of this venerable man.

THE KYOTO MAN
I know the hatred of women. I know
that. But I assure you, in every
instance, it has been a simple
case of mistaken masculinity.

AT SOME POINT HE MENTIONS HOW MANY TIMES HE HAS TURNED
INTO KYOTO, SIGHING, AS IF THE ELOCUTION HURTS HIM, OR
BORES HIM, OR PERPLEXES HIM, OR ALL OF THESE THINGS.
AND AFTER HE TURNS INTO KYOTO, THE CAMERA PROPELS UP AND
DOWN THE EMPTY STREETS OF THE CITY, AIMLESSLY, PAUSING
TO CAPTURE THE UNCANNY RESONANCE OF CERTAIN TEMPLES,
INDUSTRIAL PLANTS AND WINDPOWERED ROTATING TOWERS, AND
IT BECOMES EVIDENT THAT THIS VERSION OF KYOTO EXISTS
IN THE NEAR FUTURE - A GEOMETRICAL PARADOX OF ABSTRACT
DIFFERENCE AND FLUID SYMMETRY - AND THEN WE REALIZE
THE CITY IS EVOLVING BEFORE OUR EYES, FROM SLOWTIME TO
FASTTIME, WITH DOMES SPROUTING UP LIKE MUSHROOMHEADS,
AND MIRRORED SPIRES PIERCING THE TENNÉ SKY...

二十八

the 8193rd time I turned into Kyoto

DEAD AIR

INFODUMP, OR, THY PILES

It was not long after he had stood in the foyer of the social theater—the first televised newscast, in fact, set the wheel in motion—that a religious fervor overcame the population. It began with the lower classes, as is customary. Lack of funding exacerbates the fear of death. Or, as Karl Marx suggests in "The Poverty of Philosophy": "From day to day it thus becomes clearer that the production relations in which the bourgeoisie moves have not a simple, uniform character, but a dual character; that in the selfsame relations in which wealth is produced, poverty is also produced; that in the selfsame relations in which there is a development of the productive forces, there is also a force producing repression; that these relations produce *bourgeois wealth*—i.e., the wealth of the bourgeois class—only by continually annihilating the wealth of the individual members of this class and by producing an ever-growing proletariat." Thus are proles more inclined to inject the opiate of the masses, albeit yuppies inexorably follow in their train. They worshipped "Superzero," as they deigned to call him—although others called him "Ur-Vishnu," and "Overglyph," and "Man Plus," and "Proust's Kraken," and so on—with madcap piety, constructing idols of him in human and metropolitan forms. And the more damage he caused, the more adamantly the masses genuflected.

INFODUMP, OR, THY PILES

If he is not God, they proclaim, then he is a superhero. The man to end all men. The destroyer of all men. Paradox of patriarchy. He possesses special abilities. If nothing else, he exhibits a psychic life of power. There is evidence. We can prove it. And if we can't prove it, we can spin it.

INFODUMP, OR, THY PILES

Considering the unwarranted value of his character, **Ira Überstein** doesn't appear often enough in this book of lies and mindscapes. His spirit lurks behind every curtain, beneath every floorboard, perpetuating makeshift bushido dreams, but his presence is shockingly restricted, arguably neglected, if not forgotten. Unforgiveable. And yet necessary. Puppeteers are puppeteers for a reason. To see the strings is only a misdemeanor. To see who pulls the strings is a felony punishable by immolation. The flames of reality lay down the law.

   Additionally: more gun-fu.

INFODUMP, OR, THY PILES

In the past and the future—*ipso facto*, the present doesn't exist—speculation persists as to the correlation between the metromorph and TCZs. Which is the chicken? Which is the egg? A protectorate of Big Bang theorists have come dangerously close to unlocking this mystery. Drawing on the expertise of tornado hunters, they "captured" a "fragment" of a TCZ as it "rolled across the landscape" and "analyzed it under a microscope." Significant turbulence marred the case study, rendering constants invariables and variables inconstant, hurling the theorists back and forth through Time and modes of fashion, and in general schizophrenizing their intellectual circuitry, powers of perception, and hermeneutics of suspicion. Nonetheless they drew some rudimentary conclusions. Above all, they detected traces of the metromorph's DNA in the "feathery parts" of the sample TCZ. This caused an upheaval. How did the Big Bang theorists know what the metromorph's DNA looked like? He had never been examined, as he had never been captured, and almost nobody could identify him; he could walk down a busy citystreet at high noon and ne'er a head would turn. The theorists proffered a "medicinal argument," claiming they had "experienced" the man→city's DNA in a collective, magic mushroom-induced hallucination. This didn't go over well either. They changed their tune, assuring the global public that they did not do drugs and in fact were all "Born-Again Inviolates." Blind Faith, not "some trippy shitstorm," led them to their hypothesis. This carried more weight with the Human Stain, although history underwent constant revision, literally, and therefore the future always-already spiraled in multiple directions. Sometimes Blind Faith worked. Usually it generated incontinence.

INFODUMP, OR, THY PILES

There is a rumor of his death. There is a rumor of his dismemberment. There is a rumor of his cremation, of his vaporization. Every rumor expels the same coda. The flakes of his flesh recompose into a molar dialectic...The sharp molecularization reverts, regresses, lapses into the city, and then he backtracks to human form, sans wounds, as perfect as any anthropomorph could hope to be, if only on a mindscreen. He can be killed but nobody can kill him.

INFODUMP, OR, THY PILES

The Stix had their origins in Japanese *yokai*, shapeshifting goblins, daemons, specters, deities, ghosts, phantasms, and other monsters that formerly existed as literary, cultural and historical icons with sliding veneers of signification, but the birth of "poltergestalt," a portmanteau technology that combined the machinery of haunting with the economics of flesh, saw the manifestation of *yokai* in the real world. Of course, they took over. All sentient organisms want to take over. During this period, reality flirted with the diegesis of a zombie film.

Nothing lasts forever. In spite of an eager penchant for self-destruction, the Human Stain can't take a hint and won't go away. In time, the *yokai*'s reign ended. The Stain rose against the enemy like a fleet of angry proles, executing them for "crimes against Bartleby." Residual *yokai* became the subjects of mad scientism, a practice that mainly produced unfathomable pain and suffering (i.e., "retribution"), but also cures for cancer and AIDS, which, on some timelines, are currently available for purchase in over-the-counter capsule form (e.g., a bottle of 40 capsules at any Allpurpose Department Warehouse runs for the price of a 2000 square foot home in a prestigious westworld suburb, a remarkable value considering that two swallows per day for twenty consecutive days guarantees an end to the affliction in 82% of affected parties. The cure can be obtained in third world, arctic, and postapocalyptic outrézones for a tremendous discount. FINE PRINT: The chances of being killed and robbed immediately following purchase exceed 95%). The Stain genetically regressed other surviving *yokai*, devolved them into proto-life forms as punishment for their insurrection, while augmenting their intellects so that they could more effektively understand and experience the nature of their ruined existence, or, in Buddhist lingo, their *dukkha*. Hence the Stix. Making them smart was a dumb thing to do. But it wasn't the first dumb thing the Stain had done, and it wouldn't be the last.

The Stix realized that they could easily reroute the Stain's aggression, and they rose against them like a fleet of angry proles…

On the ground, there were bloody, savage hand-to-hand skirmishes; in space, starships destroyed one another with doomsday machines and wavemotion guns. Once the Stain had been sufficiently enslaved, a Dark Age crippled the socius. Earth had never harbored more intelligent beings than the Stix, and the Stain knew it, and the Stain decided not to write anything down or even draw any pictures, reverting to a primitive culture of sheer oral transmission. Simple logic. Future generations and (d)evolutions did not deserve to know their business. Nobody could be smarter than the Stain—period. (NOTE: A similar outlook belonged to the modernists of the twentieth century, who dared to call themselves "modernists," agreeing that nobody could or would be more modern than them.) And so they dispossessed their successors of a sense of history, and by the time their successors understood that they lived in a prison of ignorance, the Stain had rallied again. They obliterated the metaphysical anomalies. "Genocide is the best pesticide," remarked the Stain.

Then the timecrashes began. Then the zoneshifts. Then a fusion of temporal and spatial malfunctions. We had no choice but to blame them on the Stix.

INFODUMP, OR, THY PILES

TCZs no longer exist. One could make that argument and defend it with textual support, just as one could make the argument that reality is a myth, an illusion, the dream of a pathological android.

More likely, TCZs simply go unnoticed. The mind doesn't work like it used to. Things change and yet things appear the same. Such ignorance mainly afflicts the few survivors that wander up and down the seashores of the future. Dazed. Schized. Fat and mad.

INFODUMP, OR, THY PILES

In due course the pharmacists attempted to win. It had nothing to do with pills—wielding pills, dispensing pills, using pills as bait, etc. They simply made a collective decision. There were enough of them, by then, and they wreaked considerable havoc, mixing and matching prescriptions until their customers didn't know tit from tat. Like all good autocracies, however, it came to a bitter and violent end, and for a while customers could not get their medication.

INFODUMP, OR, THY PILES

In *Bullitt* (1968), Steve McQueen's character drives a 1968 Mustang Fastback.

INFODUMP, OR, THY PILES

This is an apocalyptic novel. This is an apoplectic novel, an anaphylactic novel. Nothing more—nothing less.

INFODUMP, OR, THY PILES

One of the wild theses in *A Brief History of the Man→City*

is the unearthly conceit that the man→city occupies ubiquity, i.e., that he has actually been encountered in opposite latitudes at the same time. An even wilder thesis has to do with the differences between western and eastern cultures. According to the author of *A Brief History*, everybody knows that the man is a westerner. And yet that which he becomes is clearly an easterner. How, the author asks, do we account for this polarization? Is it a mere allegory for the banal clash of self vs. other? Or does the metromorphosis exhibit a deeper, meatier significance, one that reveals certain diagnostics of civilization? Either way, I expect the worst, and I hope for the best. I am serious. I am perpetually, incurably serious. People live and die and are forgotten. Hence the drama of human existence.

二十九

the 9998th time I turned into Kyoto

WANTED SIGN

WANTED

FOR MURDER, METROMORPHIA AND CRIMES AGAINST THE REPUBLIK

THE KYOTO MAN

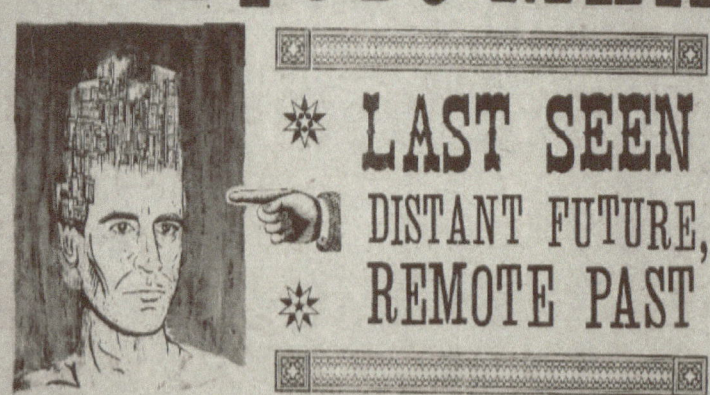

✦ LAST SEEN
DISTANT FUTURE, REMOTE PAST

CIVILIZATION APPROACHES THE FINISH LINE. HUMANITY'S PAST, PRESENT & FUTURE LINGERS ON THE THRESHOLD OF MYTHOLOGY. HISTORY EVAPORATES. VIRTUALLY NOONE HAS EVER EXISTED. SOON ALL THAT WILL BE LEFT ARE A FEW STRAGGLED BODY ARTISTS AND MEN OF ILL CONSEQUENCE. WE MUST APPREHEND THE ANAMOLY, DEAD OR ALIVE. WE MUST SAVE OURSELVES FROM INEVITABILITY.

the 9000th time I turned into Kyoto

CRITERION PROSE

Scikungfi fight. In the technologized vein of Antonio Inoki vs. Mohammed Ali. In the future. Inoki damages Ali's legs as Ali fails to deflect the rapidfire kicks…

Jiendo: Dr. Weißerwal succumbed to "Ishmael," the patient. The doktor had never lost a match except to the sensei that trained him. He was a born fighter, a born winner.

After producing several compound fractures in his legbones, "Ishmael" shattered Dr. Weißerwal's windpipe and almost killed him. Paramedics couldn't fully restore him and he had to be put on life support.

During the operation, "Ishmael" showered and gave himself a manicure, pushing back cuticles with the tip of a martini stirrer…

"Ishmael" sat on the edge of a chaise. Two orderlies wheeled Dr. Weißerwal into the office on a rollaway bed. He spoke through an electrolarynx taped to his neck.

"Let's talk about your masculinity," fizzled Dr. Weißerwal.

"No need," replied "Ishmael." "You'll scarcely meet a man more masculine than me."

"All right. Let's talk about your traumatic kernels."

"My kernels are like ball bearings—smooth and round, mirrored and shining, innocent and untouched. They know no trauma."

"All right. Let's talk about something else. Let's talk about…coitus?"

"I haven't engaged in coitus for years. I'd be challenged to describe the act of coitus. I might go so far as to argue that the act of coitus is a government conspiracy created to disenfranchise the masses. It's a myth. It's a legend."

"Your parents?"

"Dead. Always dead."

"Your job? What is it you do for a living?"

"This and that."

"And do you have any hobbies? What do you do in your spare time?"

"This and that. This and that."

"All right then. What about suicide? We've never talked about suicide. Have you ever wanted to kill yourself?"

"I once had a bad 24-hour flu. I threw up every fifteen minutes. After the thirtieth time I threw up, I remember wishing that I were dead. I didn't want to kill myself. But I wanted to be dead."

"Ah."

"Ishmael" stood, walked over to the doktor and mopped off his brow with a cold, moist sponge.

"That feels good," said Dr. Weißerwal. "I appreciate it."

"Here's a pill. Take this."

"Thank you." *GLP.*

"My turn." *GLP. GLP. GLP. GLP. GLP. GLP. GLP. GLP. GLP. GLP. GLP. GLP. GLP. GLP. GLP. GLP. GLP. GLP. GLP. GLP. GLP. GLP. GLP. GLP.* "Ahh."

Dr. Weißerwal said, "That's better."

"Yes," "Ishmael" agreed. "Much better."

"What were we talking about?"

"My problem."

"Yes. What is your problem?"

"I don't have a problem."

"I see. Why are you here, then?"

"Because we've lost all sense of history. We envision the past at whim, not as it was, but as we want it to be, or as we think it was, not how it actually was, and is, and will be. And the loss of history authorizes a negation of the future. It began with the mediatization of reality and the flesh, this loss. Pop culture, etc. Stupid teenaged assholes prancing across a stage. Shitforbrained audiences. Epidemic redneckery. Then the spectacle became the real. Coupled with the slow rape of the natural world?" "Ishmael" shrugged.

Dr. Weißerwal's breathing machine whirred. "That's not your problem. That's whitewash. History at large doesn't matter vis-à-vis your subjective complications. The only history that really matters is the history of your selfhood. Period."

"The history of my selfhood is produced by my interactions with other selfhoods all of which are produced by their own histories and their own senses of history at large. Fuck you."

The doktor remained silent for a long time. At last he said, "Soon I will die. You won't have anybody to talk to. What will you do then, 'Ishmael'?"

"I'll be all right. I'm indestructible now. I can tear my arm off and it grows back. I can do anything. And I'm famous. I'm a celebrity. Everybody knows my name."

The breathing machine stopped. "Damn this thing," wheezed Dr. Weißerwal. "Can you fix this damned thing?"

"I wish I could. I'll see if there's a technician in the hallway."

"I would very much like that. A technician would be useful at this juncture."

"I have to go." He walked to the door.

"When you have to go…you have to go."

"Thanks for all your help." He put his hand on the doorknob.

"I'm glad I could help."

"You're a good therapist. The best." He turned the doorknob.

"Thera. Pist. The…best."

He paused. He listened to the doktor's sterterous breaths. He wouldn't last much longer. Maybe only a few seconds.

"I hurt. Inside," said "Ishmael."

"I know. Y-you'll be…ok."

"Goodbye, Dr. Weißerwal." He opened the door.

"Goodbye. Goodbye…sir."

"Call me 'Ishmael.'" He walked through the door.

"Y-y-y…yes…'Ish-ma-el.' 'Ish…'"

He closed the door behind him.

✝—

the asooth time i turned into kyoto

CORMAC MCCARTHY PROSE

The *daikaiju* stood and put one leg forward and the sky behind him turned different shades of orange like a patchwork of autumn leaves. The city beneath him, beyond him. Dreamscape. He loomed over the world naked and staring at the atmosphere. Creosote skin. Something pulsed within the obscure silhouette of his body. Wild spirals and the engines of night. His fingers were spread apart. He reached forward with one arm and bent his left leg, flexing the calf muscle, to maintain balance when the metromorphosis began and bright yellow flames exploded from his palm, his shoulders, his thighs. The muscles in his chest and groin burned like embers. Triangulation of hearts. Something else. He didn't fight it. The steeple of a pagoda erupted from his left shoulderblade and complemented the pagoda beneath him rising out of the trees. Gossamer skyscraper in the remote distance. There wasn't anything in his face. A blank, black screen. Vague impression of an ocular cavity. All of this was frozen in time and above the *daikaiju* in sharp white letters hung the signature of his identity and beneath him the author of his pain.

三十二

the 10001st time I turned into Kyoto
CRITERION PROSE

A pale red sun stained the white screen of sky. Beneath the sun—vastness…

The outréman lay unconscious for hours as earthsalt sifted across his febrile, naked body. When he awoke, he felt good. Refreshed.

He stood.

Hypotension. Images of ultraviolence flitted across the mindscreen. Mnemonic remnants. He witnessed the demolition of infinite bodies sliced in half from skull to coccyx, brains and blood and organs erupting in an apocryphal fête. Strands of viscera. ゴア.

A Molotov cocktail struck a bystander in the face. Smash. Blam. The bystander's skin dribbled from the screaming bone.

Neosporin.

The wind crossed the brown land. He didn't hear it but he felt it and it drew him out of the reverie.

It was the violet hour.

The world was flat. The world had been flattened. As if a biblical steamroller had rolled across the landscape, leveling everything in its path—trees, mountains, men—all of it pulverized and spread across the planet like tarmac. Like a glacier. A scorched glacier. It went on and on and on. Cracks extended in terminal spokes from the outréman's feet and widened into gullies, ditches, *canali*. Faraway the ruptured topography yawned into deep canyons that no one would ever see or experience or fathom.

What would he do now?

Start over. Begin again. *Heitan*. Every day is a new day, every breath a new breath. And yet beginnings always come to an end. *Jiendo*. The end.

He closed his eyes.

Mnemonic turbines. The solodex…rotors spun like a roulette wheel…

He recalled…his mother. It was dark and he was scared. She sat on the edge of the bed and ran her fingers over the skin of his face. "This is the life force," she whispered. "It protects you. It energizes you. It flows from your core into eternity. Can you feel it? Don't worry, honey. Childhood is a dream. Sometimes it's a good dream and sometimes it's a bad one. I know you'll wake up. I have confidence in you. Feel the life force. Someday you'll grow up. Someday you'll set the world on fire. You are capable. You are talented. You can do whatever you want to do. The life force says so." She stroked his arms and his chest and then his face again. He listened to her voice. He felt the wind. "The wind." "Her voice." The dirt. "Her voice." Earth. Space. A passageway. "Her voice, her voice." April. Beneath the dry thunder. "A way a lone a last a loved along the." Mother. Mommy.

A kiss goodnight.

三十三

the nth time i turned into kyoto

CRITERION PROSE

INFODUMP, OR, THY PILES

With the exception of temple podia, castle foundations, pagodas, and analogous structures, Japanese architecture elides stone in favor of wood, tendered and cured with varying degrees of skill, with screens made of paper, mats made of straw, walls made of plaster and clay, and roofs made of reeds and wooden shingles or planks or tile. This elision differentiates it from Western architecture more than any other feature. The future unravels in infinite platitudes and the future of Kyoto is no exception. Soon it will be like all of the others, alone and singular, rendering the city Everything. Or it will become a simple Man of the Crowd distinguished by ferroconcrete streets and spidersteel towers. Nobody will know who (re)constructed it. Nobody leaves their conapts. No reason. The Grocery Store comes to them.

The city glints like tinfoil beneath the purple night sky. A rainbow arches out of Sector Z into an obsidian cloud. Poisonous black vapors curl from the mouths of tall, thin, mirror-plated chimneys and smokestacks. Nobody has lived here for years. Centuries. Nobody has ever lived here. And yet the city was born, and it has continued to evolve.

Long ago, it existed purely as glass, every countertop, every wall, every building a paradigm of geometric efficiency and simplicity, a congress of inflexible straight lines. Years later, glass fell into a stupor and the city converted to sheer brownstone, its bulwarks and fortifications solid brick. In some areas buildings lay in ruins while down the block stood cliffs of edifice in which elevators rose and fell without the slightest turbulence. They were soon replaced—i.e., "strangled"—by great "anthills" or "fungus chimneys" that stood over two miles high. These well-ventilated eco-structures housed insects and human beings with identical efficacy. Acceleration of technicity…a tangle of slidewalks and superhighways and slatstreets draped over the rooftops, festooned among the empty hard spaces…This led to a moment during which the city flickered between realistic construction and cartoon animétion. And then the Romantic period: how the overflowing streets unfolded into a ballast of itinerant vehicles and vulgar forms of houses and pavement that denied the still mountains. And then the Neuromantic period: flickering corporate arcologies, shoals of white Styrofoam, towering hologram logos, vidbuildings on which Coca-Cola geishas invited thirsty consumers to drink themselves into carbonated oblivion. Glowglobes illuminated the night in a vast lattice of virtual fire. The shadows of noospheric flâneurs paraded across the arcade walls and threatened to blackout the various wares for sale beyond the store windows. Exegetical cragmentation. Bonsai trees pushed through cracks in the sidewalks, unleashing their buds, crawling up and down the scaffolding of ancient fortresses. The bounty hunters are dead. The mad scientists are dead. The shitty parents are dead. Gone. Bleached ribs of prehistoric, towering leviathans. Churchspires expanded and climbed from the bones like yeast. Bituminous stonework gleamed in the rain. As the rivers boiled over, as the gardens spit pinecones and wasp husks, intricate railways inflated on the body of the city like varicose veins, culminating in a great aortic pulse. Row-houses. *Minka*. In this axonometric diagram, a prefecture comes to life, corpuscles gushing into the excavation and producing a fine and massive erection. The features: central square ceiling, hidden rafters, cantilevers, bottle-shaped struts, shrimplike rainbow beams, carved plinths, an altar, hisashi, raigobashira, and the core. Semiotic poltergeists hemorrhaged from the core and spiraled outwards until the dogged conurbation bore a hauntology incited by its own crackedopen selfhood. There is nothing worse than selfhood gone awry. The litany of Ego has no boundaries; it clambers up and down, up and down, up and down the xylophone at its leisure and only sleeps when it passes out from drink and fatigue. Unfortunately Ego always awakens.

Later, after the sun imploded, the shadow of a Slender Man, arms outstretched, head thrown back, lingered in the doorway. I could almost feel myself casting it.

In the end...but there is no end. The cityscape bucks and swerves like an old rollercoaster ride, through subterranean tunnels and across the sky, until it encrusts the world like an exoskeleton, squeezing magma from the peachpit. Lava erupts into space in obscene bursts...The world is not enough. Scotch is not enuff, altho it shud be...Especially gud scotch. Oban. Isle of Skye. But even rail scotch shud do. It dont...The only option is dissemination. The only option is to overcome the self. The demonic limits of the self. To wield the illimitable strength of origin, of futurity...I was a boy and now I am a man. I am a man and now I am a monster. But the drugs have worn off and now I can experience the nicotine. I have been deceiving my dopamine receptors. Now I am back to normal.

Normal is the stuff of legend.

三十四

the last time I turned into Kyoto

CRITERION PROSE

Two figures collided on the outskirts of an Unreal City. It was dawn. Brown fog loomed over the cold grass. Corpses littered the outréscape, decaying in a timelapse of molten flesh.

The figures enacted signature maneuvers and singular resilience in the wake of token suckerpunches. When the fight was over, they faced one another and shook hands like gentlemen.

"Tell me everything," said one man. "Be honest."

"I will," said the other man. "I always tell the truth. This is how it began…I fell in love with a woman. Her name was Sasha Crack. We were only nineteen. We loved each other and then we fell apart. I grew older. Then, last week, or last month, or thereabouts, I saw her again. It had been over forty years. We talked about the old days. I asked Sasha if she remembered the first time I kissed her. She didn't. She asked me if I remembered the first time I kissed her. I couldn't. We began to fight. We fell apart again…It was as if that first kiss had never happened. And it didn't happen. When memory fails, history evaporates. Signification dies; the monkey loses its Kong. A terrifying lack. I want that kiss back in my head. Nostalgia for nostalgia—it wounds me. Defines me. My whole life stems from an nth degree of meaning. All this happened in the caves of steel. No. The caves of ice. Yes. My eyes flashed, my hair floated in the maelstrom. I drank the milk of paradise from the teat of a dead goat. I—"

"Wait," interrupted the first man. "I think I hear something. Listen…Do you hear it?"

With great difficulty, the other man broke the iron grip of his ego. "I don't hear anything."

"Listen." He pointed.

"I don't hear anything. What is it?"

The man lowered his arm. "The sound of transformation."

There was a long, iconic pause.

Then, at last:

"I hear it," said the other man. "I can hear it now."

In the distance—the sky, the surf, the wind in my hair...

tHE KYOtO MAN

D. Harlan Wilson is an award-winning, critically acclaimed novelist, short story writer, literary critic, editor, and English prof. He is www.thekyotoman.com.